# CORA SANDEL: SELECTED SHORT STORIES

# CORA SANDEL:

## SELECTED SHORT STORIES

### translated by Barbara Wilson

The Seal Press

This book was published with the help of the National Endowment for the Arts, the Norwegian Cultural Council and the Nordmanns Forbundet.

The photograph on the cover is of Cora Sandel in Paris in 1910, courtesy of Erik Jönsson.
Cover design by Deborah Brown
Text design by Barbara Wilson
Composition by Walker & Swenson

Published by The Seal Press
312 S. Washington
Seattle, WA 98104

Library of Congress Cataloging-in-Publication Data

Sandel, Cora, 1880-1974
    Cora Sandel: selected short stories.
    1. Sandel, Cora, 1880-1974 — Translations, English.
I. Title.
PT8950.F2A28    1985        839.8'2372        85-22295
ISBN 0-931188-31-8
ISBN 0-931188-30-X (pbk.)

First edition, November 1985

Printed in the United States of America

# Contents

# Cora Sandel — Life and Work

1880    Born Sara Fabricius December 20 in Kristiania (pres-
        ent-day Oslo), the eldest daughter of a middle class
        family. Her father is a sea captain who later enters
        government service as an administrator.

1892    Moves to Tromsø, high above the Arctic Circle, with
        her parents and two younger brothers.

1899    Her earliest ambition is to become an artist. Studies
        briefly in Kristiania with the painter Harriet Backer.

1905    Returns to Kristiania to study painting.

1906    Leaves for Paris to continue her studies. Intending to
        stay a year, she remains fifteen, becoming part of a
        circle of struggling expatriate artists. Is influenced by
        Colette, especially by her novel, *The Vagabond*, and
        years later writes of its effect on her: "I read breath-
        lessly, without a break, and knew the first stirrings of
        desire, of the need to write myself. It was possible to
        do it that way, so bluntly and without flourishes, so
        condensed and at the same time so natural. That's
        how it could be, without a flabby sentence, without
        a superfluous word, tightly fitting the theme like a
        skin and never forced."

1913    Marries the up-and-coming Swedish sculptor Anders
        Jönsson, whose large marble groups are somewhat
        reminiscent of Rodin.

1913-15   Lives with her husband in Florence on his grant from the Swedish government.

1917   Son Erik is born.

1918   Paints her last picture; begins to write in Brittany.

1921   Moves with her husband and son to Sweden, outside Stockholm. Her canvases are used as wrapping for her husband's sculpture. In her bags are notes for a novel based on her childhood.

1922   Separates from her husband and travels to Tromsø to teach. Her first story is published under the pseudonym Cora Sandel. "The Ways of Love" is published in a Norwegian literary magazine and brings her to the attention of the editor of Gyldendal publishers.

1923   Returns to Sweden, where she remains most of the rest of her life. She continues to consider herself a Norwegian author, however, and all her works are written in Norwegian.

1926   Divorced from Anders Jönsson. Custody battle over their son. Her first novel, *Alberta and Jacob (Alberta og Jakob)* is published to critical and public acclaim.

1927   *A Blue Sofa (En blå sofa)*. Stories.

1931   *Alberta and Freedom (Alberte og frihet)*. Second volume of Alberta trilogy.

1932   *Carmen and Maja (Carmen og Maja)*. Stories.

1935   *Thank You, Doctor (Mange takk, doktor)*. Stories.

1939   *Alberta Alone (Bare Alberte)*. Final volume of trilogy.

1943   The story "To Lukas" is published in an anthology of Norwegian writers in exile.

1945   *Krane's Cafe (Kranes konditori)*. Novel. *Animals I've Known (Dyr jeg har kjennt)*. Stories.

1947   *Krane's Cafe* is dramatized for theater in Oslo.

1949   *Figures on a Dark Wall (Figurer på mørk bunn)*. Stories.

1951   *Krane's Cafe* is filmed.

1952   Her translation of *The Vagabond* into Norwegian is published, with an introduction that shows the importance of Colette to Sandel's life and work.

1958   *The Leech (Kjøp ikke Dondi)*. Novel.

1960   *Our Difficult Life (Vårt vanskelige liv)*. Selection of previously published stories from various collections, chosen in conjunction with Odd Solumsmoen.

1972   Exhibition in Sweden of thirty of her early paintings. *Alberta and Freedom* is filmed for Scandinavian television.

1973   *The Child Who Loved Roads (Barnet som elsket veier)*. A book of previously uncollected stories and sketches, edited by Steinar Gimnes.

1974   Cora Sandel dies April 3.

## Work Available in English

*Alberta and Jacob; Alberta and Freedom; Alberta Alone*. Translated by Elizabeth Rokkan. Originally published in 1962, 1963 and 1965 by Peter Owen, London, and by The Women's Press, London, in 1980. Current U.S. edition: University of Ohio Press, 1984.

*Krane's Cafe*. Translated by Elizabeth Rokkan. Originally published in 1968 by Peter Owen, London. Current U.S. edition: University of Ohio Press, 1985.

*The Leech*. Translated by Elizabeth Rokkan. Originally published in 1960 by Peter Owen, London.

# Introduction

I LIKE TO WALK and I suspect that Cora Sandel did too. Her stories are filled with women and children and men on the move. From the young girl in "The Child Who Loved Roads," who makes up stories while investigating country highways and byways, to the solitary Mrs. Arnold of "A Mystery," who escapes her benefactors to roam the forest paths, the typical Sandel character seems to regard walking as a kind of thought process, a rumination; restless, inspired, dreamy. Likewise, whether Sandel is telling the story the way she remembers it or letting her characters play it out themselves, her observant eye, her perfect ear, and her poignant sense of humor give each of her stories the characteristics of a good walk, a walk that sometimes circles neatly back on itself and sometimes covers a great deal of ground in a short time, to end far from where it began.

In the English-speaking world Cora Sandel is best known for her Alberta trilogy. The books have rarely been out of print in their English translation and, in recent years, have been recognized as feminist classics. Sandel's semi-autobiographical story of a woman's long struggle to define herself as a writer has parallels with the work of many twentieth-century writers, but her particular emphasis on the difficult economics of being a woman, especially a mother, is comparatively rare. Like Jean Rhys, a writer to whom she bears some resemblance, Sandel was eminently gifted at dissecting the unequal power relations between men and women. Unlike Rhys' heroines, however, Alberta fights against her passivity and ultimately finds her freedom and herself.

In Norway and Sweden Cora Sandel is considered a major short story writer as well as a novelist. Her short fiction has long been recognized for its lyric intensity and stylistic economy and is often anthologized. More recently, Scandinavian women critics have been rediscovering the feminist content of her work, and she has been the subject of several books and numerous articles.

The stories in this translation follow, with one addition and two omissions, a selection made by Odd Solumsmoen with Cora Sandel's help, and are drawn from her four collections. *Our Difficult Life* was published in 1960 and is still the most widely available edition of her stories in Norway. I have also included the title story from *The Child Who Loved Roads*, a book of previously uncollected prose that came out in 1973.

Solumsmoen and Sandel arranged the stories chronologically, according to the book in which they first appeared, and I have followed that order. Five of the stories ("The Ways of Love," "Mother," "Larsen's," "Bernhardt" and "Shit-Katrine") are from *A Blue Sofa* and are good examples of Sandel's early condensed and occasionally elliptic style. "Klara" and "A Mystery" from *Carmen and Maja*, published the year after *Alberta and Freedom*, show her increasing concern with the sexual double-standard, as well as with the difficulties of financial survival for women on their own.

These two stories are, additionally, fine character portraits, a mode that Sandel, the former painter, was to utilize successfully in many of the stories taken from *Thank You, Doctor*. Lola, the artist's model, Hval, the biggest gold buyer at the auction hall, and Tora and Adele, the quarreling but complementary sisters, are all lively and unforgettable characters, as is the parrot Papen. Like Colette, Sandel loved animals, and her fourth collection was entitled *Animals I've Known*. "Papen" is as touching and unsentimental a study of loneliness as any Sandel has created.

Cora Sandel's views of marriage and male-female relationships are often bleak. Separated by personal and social misunderstandings as well as different values and needs, her men and women continue to seek each other blindly and hurtfully in such stories as "Thank You, Doctor," "The Child," and "The Flight to America." Sandel's struggle for custody of her son finds echoes in the latter two stories, as she records the loss children suffer when their parents are estranged.

The first and the last stories in this collection were written in the 1940s. In them Sandel returns to the elliptic style that marked her earlier writing; this time, however, with a surer hand and broader focus. "The Child Who Loved Roads" is a perfect introduction to Sandel's recurring theme of solitary independence, while "To Lukas" strikes a more somber note of wartime loss and loneliness. This story is set in Stockholm between 1940 and 1943. Unlike most European countries, including German-occupied Denmark and Norway, Sweden was neutral during World War II. Sandel's ambivalent feelings about living in a country providing a safe haven for thousands of refugees while furnishing Germany with raw materials for its war machine emerge in this haunting series of unmailed letters from a Czechoslovakian refugee to her husband.

I have tried as much as possible to keep to Cora Sandel's style and to reproduce her very subtle sense of irony in English. There are two aspects of the translation that need some mention. Sandel frequently wrote in the present tense, or a combination of the present and past. It was a deliberate choice and one that I have tried to respect, knowing how furious Sandel became over previous translations of her novels (to the extent of refusing royalties). I have, however, occasionally opted for overall consistency when, because of change in mood or emphasis, the tenses weave back and forth in a somewhat bewildering fashion.

Second, I've had to make my own choices about which pronoun to use in several of the stories about children and animals. Sandel uses "det" or "it" to refer to "the child," for example, something that is obviously not acceptable in English. That's a pity in some ways, for one of the striking aspects of Sandel's authorship is her tendency to universalize. Very often her characters are not even named; they are "the lady," "the mother," "the girl," or simply "he" and "she" and "it," intentionally and eternally emblematic.

Cora Sandel was a writer who perfected each sentence and carefully shaped each story. As a fiction writer, I have been awed by her mastery of the craft and inspired in my own work. As well as a stylist, however, she was an instinctively radical story-teller who wrote with compassion and humor about the oppressed, the marginal and the simply lonely. An undercurrent of anger runs through much of her writing, an anger directed toward hypocrisy and injustice of any kind. At the same time Sandel's characters are never victims. Sometimes independent, sometimes trapped, never quite extinguished, they continue to struggle to keep their dignity and to win their freedom. It has been, finally, Cora Sandel's tenderness and strength that have sustained me in the difficult art of translating her stories.

*Barbara Wilson*
*Seattle, Washington*
*August 1985*

# Acknowledgements

A number of people have generously shared their time and knowledge with me to make these translations possible. I would especially like to thank Ida Munck for her friendship and for inspiring this work, Tiina Nunnally and Janet Rasmussen for their valuable suggestions, and Sally Brunsman and Faith Conlon of Seal Press for their help with the final draft. Erik Jönsson has been supportive and generous with information and criticism from the beginning. Katherine Hanson, a fine scholar and excellent translator herself, not only taught me a great deal about translation, but also let me swim off her houseboat in Portage Bay. I would also like to thank the Columbia Translation Center, the Norsk Kulturråd, the Nordmanns Forbundet and the National Endowment for the Arts for their financial support.

# CORA SANDEL:
## SELECTED SHORT STORIES

# The Child Who Loved Roads

MOST OF ALL she loved roads with the solitary track of a horse down the middle and with grass between the wheel ruts. Narrow old roads with lots of bends and nobody else around and here and there a piece of straw perhaps, fallen from a load of hay. The child turned springy and light as air on them, filled with happiness at breaking free, at existing. Behind each bend waited unknown possibilities, however many times you'd gone down the road. You could make them up yourself if nothing else.

Down the highway she walked, dragging her feet in dust and gravel. Dust and gravel were among the bad things in life. You got tired, hot, heavy, longed to be picked up and carried.

Then suddenly the narrow old road was there, and the child began to run, leaping high with happiness.

She hadn't been so tired after all, the grown-ups said. There's a lot grown-ups don't understand. You have to give up explaining anything to them and take them as they are, an inconvenience, for the most part. No one should grow up. No, children should stay children and rule the whole world. Everything would be more fun and a lot better then.

Early on the child learned that it was best to be alone on the road. A good ways in front of the others anyway. Only then did you come to know the road as it really was, with its marks of wheels and horses hooves, its small, stubborn stones sticking up, its shifting lights and shadows. Only then did you come to know the fringes of the road, warm from sun and greenness, plump and furry with wild chervil and lady's mantle – altogether a strange and wonderful world unto itself, where you could wander free as you pleased, and everything was good, safe, and just the way you wanted it.

At least it was in the summer. In winter the road was something else entirely. In the twilight of a snow-gray day your legs could turn to lead, everything was so sad. You never seemed to get any further; there was always a long ways to go. The middle of the road was brown and ugly, like rice pudding with cinnamon on it, a dish that grew in her mouth and that she couldn't stand. People and trees stood out black and sorrowful against the white. You did have the sledding hill, the field with deep snow for rolling on, the courtyard for building forts and caves, the skis without real bindings. For small children shouldn't have real bindings, the grown-ups said; they could fall and break their legs. In the twilight everything was merely sad, and nothing about it could compare to the roads in summer.

To be let loose on them, without a jacket, without a hat, *bare*, that was life the way it should be. Only one thing compared to it, the hills at the big farm, where she was often a guest.

There were paths bordered with heather and crowberry leading up to views over the blue fjord and to a light, never-still breeze that tickled your scalp. White stone protruded from the heather and the path. At the bottom of the hill you found wild strawberries, higher up blueberries, not just a few either, and bilberries. On top lay the crowberries in patches like large carpets.

The child could pass hours lying on her stomach near a bush, stuffing herself, and at the same time thinking of all sorts of things. She possessed an active imagination, seldom longed for company and could sometimes fly into a rage if she got it.

"You're so contrary," said the grown-ups. "Can't you be nice and sweet like the others, just a little? You should be thankful anyone wants to be with you," they said.

"It won't be easy for you when you're older," they also said.

The child forgot it as soon as it was said. She ran off to the road or the paths and remembered nothing so unreasonable, so completely ridiculous.

One road went from the house on the big farm, went along the garden where huge old red currant bushes hung over the picket fence, casually offering their magnificence; the road went across the fields, bordered by thin young trees, made a leap over a hill and swung two times like an S before it wandered out in the world and became one with the boring highway.

The child's own road, newly taken possession of summer after summer. Here no one came running after you, here you could wander without company. Nothing could happen but the right things. If anyone came driving or riding it was uncles, aunts or the farmboy. They saw you from a long distance away, they stopped; if they came by wagon you got a ride to the farm.

Here and on the hills were where the stories came into being, short ones and long ones. If they didn't look like they were living up to their promise, you just stopped and started a new one.

A place in life where freedom had no boundaries. Very different from what the grown-ups meant when they said, "in this life," or "in this world," and sighed. They also said, "in this difficult life." As if to make things as nasty as possible.

Being together with someone — that was sometimes fun and sometimes not at all. You couldn't explain why or why not; it was part of everything you imagined and that you'd never dream of talking to grown-ups about. On the contrary, you held tightly to it, like someone insisting on something wrong they've done. Maybe it was "wrong"; maybe it was one of those things that ought to be "rooted out of you." Or at best to laugh about a little, to whisper over your head.

"Constructive" it wasn't, in any case. They were always talking about the necessity of doing "constructive things."

It could be fun, when Alette came, Letta. She was a redhead, freckled, full of laughter, easy to get along with. At

her house, at the neighboring farm, was a chest in the loft, full
of old-fashioned clothes. Dresses in wonderful light colors,
flounce after flounce on the wide tarlatan skirts, a name that
was far prettier than, for example, blue cotton cambric. A
man's suit, yellow knee breeches and a green coat with gold
buttons, an unbelievable costume that didn't look like anything
the uncles wore. A folding parasol, a whole collection of odd
hats. To dress up in all that, strut around in it, stumble in the
long skirts, mimic the grown-ups and make them laugh where
they sat on the garden steps, was fun enough for a while. But
it was nothing to base a life on.

For that you could only use the roads, the paths and the
hills.


Grown-up, well, you probably had to turn into one.
Everyone did; you couldn't avoid it.

But like some of them? Definitely not.

In the first place the child was going to run her whole life,
never do anything so boring as walk slowly and deliberately.
In the second and third place...

The grown-ups didn't have much that was worthwhile. It
was true they got everything they wanted, could buy themselves things they wanted and go to bed when they felt like it,
eat things at the table that children didn't get — all the best
things, in short. They could command and scold, give canings
and presents. But they got long skirts or trousers to wear and
then they *walked. Just* walked. You had to wonder if it had
something to do with what was called Confirmation, if there
wasn't something about it that injured their legs. There probably was, since they hid them and walked. They *couldn't* run
any longer. Even though — you saw them dance; you saw them
play "Widower Seeks A Mate" and "Last Pair Out."

Maybe it was their minds something was wrong with?

Everything truly fun disappeared from their lives, and
they let it happen. None of them rebelled. On the contrary,
they grew conceited about their sad transformation. Was there

anything so conceited as the big girls when they got long skirts and put up their hair!

They walked, they sat and embroidered, sat and wrote, sat and chatted, knitted, crocheted. Walked and sat, sat and walked. Stupid, they were so stupid!

Trailing skirts were dangerous. She'd have to watch out, when the time came. Run away maybe.

At home, in the city street, were the mean boys.

Really big boys, the kind who were practically uncles, were often nice. They were the ones who organized the big circus in the empty lot, with trapeze artists, clowns and tickets that the grown-ups bought in complete seriousness: parquet circle, first class, second class. A ringmaster in a tuxedo went around the circus ring and cracked his long whip at the horses doing tricks. A true circus, so to speak, except that the horses consisted of two boys under a blanket that sometimes sagged in the middle. But that was easy to overlook.

The big boys arranged competition races in the winter, saw to it that you got new skis and real bindings; they were pillars of support. One of them once got up and lambasted his sister, who had tattled on him. A bunch of lies, made up, shameful, that you just had to sit there and take, for you didn't get anywhere saying it wasn't true.

They were pillars all the same.

But there was a half-grown kind, a mean kind, that made such a racket. They ran back and forth with wooden bats in their hands and the balls shot between them like bullets. In the winter they threw hard snowballs, and if anyone had put up an especially fine fort anywhere, they came rushing down in a crowd and stormed it, left it destroyed. Sometimes they threatened you with a beating. For no reason, just to threaten. The child was deathly afraid of them, took any roundabout way she could to avoid them; she would rather be too late for dinner.

Sometimes she *had* to come through enemy lines to get home. With her heart in her throat, with her head bowed as if in a storm, she sneaked sideways along the walls of the houses. The taunts rained down.

One day a boy of that sort came after the child, grabbed her arm, squeezed it hard and said, "You know what you are? Do you?"

No answer.

"You're just a girl. Go home where you belong."

Hard as a whip the words struck the child. Just a girl — *just.* From that moment she had a heavy burden to bear, one of the heaviest, the feeling of being something inferior, of being born that way, beyond help.

With such a burden on your back the world becomes a different place for you. Your sense of yourself begins to change.

But the roads remained an even bigger consolation than before. On them even "just a girl" felt easy, free and secure.

The child was one of those who feels sorry. For skinny horses and horses who got the whip, for cats who looked homeless, for children who were smaller than she was and who didn't have mittens in winter, for people who just generally looked poor, and for drunken men.

Why she was so sorry for drunken men was never clear. They'd drunk hard liquor; they could have left it alone. They were their own worst enemies, the grown-ups explained; if things went so badly for them it was their own fault.

In the child's eyes they were nothing but helpless. They tumbled here and there; sometimes they fell down and re-mained lying there — the policeman came and dragged them off roughly. Sorry for them, she was sorry for them; they couldn't help it, they couldn't help it for anything, however they'd come to be that way. They were like little children who can't walk on their own and do things wrong because they don't know any better.

The child cried herself to sleep at times on account of the drunkards. And on account of the horses, cats and poor people. Once you're like that, you don't have it easy. The cats she could have taken home if it hadn't been for the grown-ups. She wasn't allowed. As if one cat more or less mattered. You were power-less, in this as in everything.

On the summertime roads you forgot your troubles. If you met poorly clad people you usually knew who they were, where they lived, that they had nicer clothes at home that they saved for Sundays. The horses you met were rounded, comfort-able, easy going. They waved their long tails up over thick haunches and grazed by the roadside as soon as they got a chance. The cats rubbed against your legs, purring loudly. Farm cats who belonged somewhere and were just out for a walk.

You hardly ever met anyone, though, whether people or animals. That was what was wonderful; it became more and more wonderful as the child grew older. She had a steadily stronger desire to keep making up stories in her head. There was no place that they came so readily as along a two-wheeled track with grass in between. Or up on the hill where the breeze brushed your scalp.


Time passed. The child ran, long braid flapping, on the roads.

If she was overtaken by the grown-ups, she heard, "You're too old now to be running like that. Soon you'll be wearing long skirts, remember. A young lady *walks*, she holds herself nicely, thinks about how she places her feet. Then she can't rush away like you do."

The child ran even faster than before. To get out of ear-shot, out of range as much as possible. Her legs had grown long; they were an advantage when she took to her heels. The braid swung, the lengthened skirt swung. The child thought — one day I won't turn around when they call, I won't wait for anyone. That might be sooner than they suspect. The roads lead much farther than I realized; they lead out into the world, away from all of them.

When she stopped, she looked around with new eyes, seeing no longer just the roadsides, but the horizons. Behind them lay what she longed for, craved: freedom.


But one of the big boys, the kind who were practically uncles, suddenly popped out of nowhere. He was Letta's cousin, had passed his high school exams, was a university student.

You didn't see much of him. Letta said he was stupid and conceited, a self-important fellow who kept to his room or with the grown-ups. He himself was definitely not all that grown up, said Letta, who remembered him in short pants, remembered that he stole apples at someone's and got a caning for it at home. That wasn't so very long ago; she'd been ten years old, on a visit to his parents. Now she was thirteen, almost fourteen.

He had a strange effect on the child; he upset her from the first moment in a way that was both painful and good. It was impossible to think of him when he was nearby and could turn up; you can't think when you're blushing in confusion. But out on the roads he crept into her thoughts to the extent that she couldn't get him out again; he took up residence there, inserted himself in the middle of an on-going story, which had to be completely changed. There was no other recourse.

The story came to be about him. He became the main character, along with herself. In spite of the fact that she didn't really know how he looked; she never quite risked looking at him. And in spite of the fact that he wore long trousers, *walked*, and consequently belonged to the poor fool category.

It was inexplicable, and she felt it as slightly shameful, a defeat. The child grew fiery red with embarrassment if he so much as made an appearance. As the misfortune was written on her face, it was necessary to avoid Letta and her family, to keep to the roads as never before.

You could go into Letta's garden without being seen.

Letta followed, full of suggestions; she wanted them to get dressed up like summers before, to make fun of the cousin, who was sitting on the steps with the grown-ups – to mimic him.

"He doesn't interest me."

"You think he interests me? That's why we can tease him a little, can't we?"

"I'm not interested in teasing such a disgusting person," explained the child, marveling at her own words.

"Come anyway, though."

"No."

"Why not?"

"Because I don't want to, that's why."

But it was a terribly empty feeling, when Letta gave up and walked away. Just to talk about him was a new and remarkable experience, was something she yearned for, wanted and had to do.


The child was beginning to *walk* on the roads. Slowly even. She stood still for long moments at a time. For no reason, to fuss with the tie on her braid, to curl the end of the braid around her fingers, to scrape her toe in the gravel, to stare out into space. She sat down in the grass by the roadside, trailed her hand searchingly around between the lady's mantle and water avens, did it over and over.

Finally her hand had found something, a four-leaf clover. Thoughtfully the child walked on with it, holding it carefully between two fingers.

"Well now, finally you're acting like a big girl," said one of the aunts, pleased. "Not a minute too soon. Good thing we don't have to nag you anymore. Good thing there's still a little hem to let out in your dress. Next week we'll get Joanna the seamstress."

Hardly was it said than the child set off at full speed, in defiance, in panic.

Without her having noticed it or understood it, she had allowed something to happen, something frightening, something detestable. Something that made *them* happy. But nothing should make them happy. For then they'd be getting you where they wanted you, a prisoner, some kind of invalid.

The child didn't hear the despairing sigh of a deeply worried grown-up. That would have made her relieved and calm.
Instead she only felt torn by life's contradictions, bewildered
and confused by them.


One day the cousin left; he was simply gone. Letta said,
Who cares, he was conceited and engaged. Secretly naturally,
but it had come out that he went around with a photograph
and a pressed flower in his wallet, and that he used to meet the
postman far down the highway. Letta's father had taken him
into the office, talked with him for a long time, pointed out
what a serious thing an engagement is, nothing for a green new
graduate. Green, that was probably a good description of him.
Anyway, his fiancée's father was nothing but a shoemaker, said
Letta. She though the cousin's parents had been alerted.
    "Imagine, engaged. Him!"
    The child stood there and felt something strange in her
face, felt herself grow pale. Not red at any rate, because then
you got hot. This was a cold feeling.
    "Well, good-bye," she said.
    "Didn't you come to stay?"
    The child was already gone, was out on the road, the good
old road with the two curves like an S, with thin young trees
along it and grass between the wheel tracks. Here was the same
sense of escape as always; here you could run, not only in
fantasy, but also free from all shame, everything deceitful that
was out after you. And that was over now.
    For it was over right away. In a short painful moment – as
when a tooth is pulled out.
    Follow the roads, never become what they call grown up,
never what they call old, two degrading conditions that made
people stupid, ugly, boring. Stay how you are now, light as a
feather, never tired, never out of breath. It came down to being
careful, not just for lenthened skirts, but also for anything like
this.
    For a moment the child stopped, fished out of her pocket

a dried four-leaf clover, tore it in pieces and let the wind take the bits.

And then she ran on, over the farmyard, right up the path to the hill, where the fresh breeze blew.

# The Ways of Love

LIFE IS STRANGE and the ways of love inscrutable. Severine has lovers.

Severine's mouth is large and toothless, with blue, outward-folding lips. It's like an enormous sinkhole in Severine's face. A stream of speech flows abundantly from it, full of coarse words.

The rest of her face is a mess of wrinkles and loose, soft bags. Hidden among them are a pair of eyes and a nose that make no impression whatsoever. It's the mouth that dominates.

On top of Severine's cranium grows an impenetrable thicket that looks like old wood shavings and is raked together at the back of her head with hairpins. It once made a shining halo around her head, a halo that can still be seen in the bleached-out photograph on the bureau in her bedroom.

Inside a sloppy blouse her sagging breasts slap together over her protruding stomach. From behind she's flat and straight with a skirt that drags. Her presence is the height of aging impudence and decay.

This is Severine.

Her main lover is Lusefilten.* Somehow, this is as it should be, for Lusefilten is a masculine counterpart to Severine and, all in all, no Adonis.

He's a dirty, seedy, crooked little man with a runny nose. Everything about Lusefilten is gray except his nose, which is

*Fleablanket. Trans.

red. For coarseness only one person can surpass him...Severine.

His business is to collect and buy up rags. Severine's is to weave the rags into mats. Rags are the linchpin of their lives, both of theirs...the rags were what brought them together. One day Lusefilten came drifting by with a sack on his back. A chat began over the coffee pot in Severine's small untidy kitchen, and two kindred souls found each other.

That repulsive and disgusting characters seek each other out is understandable and human. What is less explicable is that Lusefilten has rivals. Not just the lame shoemaker...no, others. Others who have full use of their limbs and who come by bicycle in the dark, who jump off and drum an agreed-upon, quiet drum roll with their fingertips on Severine's door.

There was a time when Lusefilten wanted to settle down, give up rags and start on glue, and just prowl around in the woods when it suited him looking for twigs for glue. But it came to nothing. Severine is a free spirit. For years men had lived for her and come long distances to see her; she wanted things to stay that way.

She didn't want anyone getting other ideas, including the pastor who once turned up to urge this strayed member of the parish back to the right path. Severine's stream of language will be stamped forever on the neighborhood's memory. The pastor retreated, followed out to the main road by Severine who, in everyone's hearing, closed her speech by announcing she wasn't such a bad person that she couldn't take pity on him when put to the test.

It was a very painful and embarrassing scene, as much for the pastor as for the good Free Church neighbor ladies who had reported Severine.

She herself kept standing in her splendid little wilderness of a neglected garden...kept standing with her hands on her hips, among the dahlias and sunflowers, looking out over the battlefield.

She stood there until everyone had withdrawn. Then she went inside and everything was the same as before.

*

On one of the neighboring farms they have a daughter who is strange. They don't dare let her out of their sight and she can't go out to work for anyone...she just stays at home. She's a pale girl with red hair and a childlike expression. She's well developed, tall, with round, maternal arms. Beautiful she's not, but she's far from the opposite.

She has a way of lying down and not getting up. A way of standing silently, staring and doing nothing. She has religious tendencies, is one of those who despairs, believing themselves damned to eternity.

Her voice is hoarse and creaky, a thin thread of a voice that seems to come from deep inside and that has exhausted itself on the long, arduous, unaccustomed way out into the world.

They say sometimes she stays up three, four nights in a row, without being able to sleep; she just paces back and forth, stopping occasionally to pray, wailing shrilly. Then someone has to keep watch and look after her, walk up and down the room at her side. They give her drops they've gotten from the doctor in town.

She was always a quiet, unobtrusive girl. For many years she was out working and was completely normal, so that no one paid her any mind: not pushy but not idle either, useful and helpful in the casual way many people are, nice and neat. She wasn't the sort to laugh too much and get out of control, not one bit a flirt.

Then some strange rumors began to go around the parish. Anonymous letters came to different people, to the son of one of the big farmers, to a field hand at another farm, and finally even to the young pastor who had taken over the calling from Severine's concerned spiritual advisor.

As the letters continued to arrive, the pastor's wife saw to it that he spoke from the pulpit about it one day. He didn't know, he said, and he didn't want to know, who in the congregation was scribbling certain things – composed partly of indecent expressions – that he was regularly finding in his postbox.

But he wanted, seriously and lovingly, to admonish the person in question to think of the Scripture words, "Woe to that man by whom the offense cometh." Finally he prayed warmly and fervently for that soul that it might win the inner peace it so plainly lacked. The congregation's ears and eyes opened wide, and a strained silence prevailed in the churchyard after the service.

But the pastor's wife succeeded in more than that. She was active; she drove around and chatted confidentially with people, got her hands on other letters, undertook comparisons. A suspicion formed, the lead followed up. It led to the modest and quiet girl with the devout parents. There was general consternation. No one wanted to believe it. Least of all the pastor.

He was forced to give in again and to go solemnly to the parents. It didn't pass unnoticed, for the farm lay high and exposed.

But that same afternoon a girl groveled before him on her knees on his office floor. He had to get two men and a sled to take her home, because she turned mad and didn't want to leave his house.

She was violent for a time. Then came the wailing piety.


On the next farm lives the lady.

She lives in a dining room she rents by the week. She keeps her toilet things on the buffet.

Weeks go by, turn into months. Autumn has come; all the summer guests have returned home. But the lady keeps living in the dining room.

She looks quite acceptable, this lady; in fact, many would say she was very attractive. She has the beauty of health...a clear skin, white teeth, rich and beautiful hair, where the gray streaks are still so fine that you'd have to get very close to see them.

In the evening when the roads are violet the lady walks along them. She walks and walks in her white homespun coat. And sometimes, when the roads are no longer violet, but only faintly lit stripes in a shadowland, sometimes the lady keeps walking. It's as if she were afraid to go in. She'll stop near a yard and stand looking over the fence. Inside, trees and plants are already living their own soundless, intense night life. People are gone, birds and insects silent, only the crickets sing in the grass. Dahlias and sunflowers turn quietly toward the September moon that sails up over a pale blue sky with a lingering splash of rose in it. Everything is so still and so strangely alive. The lady stands there until she grows cold from the dew, then she goes on her way.

Inside the garden, in the house, the lamps are lit. People are moving around inside and have other things to do than to look at the moon. They pass busily by the windows. You can hear them talking and laughing. There are lots of them, having a cozy, cheerful time. A small smiling child is passed from arm to arm inside. But whether the lady is looking at all that or just at the garden is hard to tell.

When she comes back to where she lives she still doesn't go into her dining room, but sits down on the front steps and leans her head against the wall, smoking cigarettes and staring at the moon. Finally she doesn't even smoke; she just sits, with a raised face and closed eyes. She probably hears the crickets then. Even after everything has become quiet she continues to sit there...each to her own.

But when she is finally in bed, they can hear her through the thin walls. There's no peace for her; she throws herself from side to side. She gets up sometimes, to leaf through the pages of books.

And sometimes the lady sobs, even groans in a muffled way.

No one wonders any longer why the lady has stayed so long. She can stay as long as she wants. No one asks for her, no one writes telling her to come now. In the busy cities full of light, where people draw together against winter like bees swarming into a hive, no one sits waiting for the lady. She is bitterly alone.

From Severine's garden comes the sound of whispers. The gate squeaks on its hinges. Severine's unbridled laughter bursts out briefly before ending in a giggle.

The strange girl prays hoarsely and pipingly. The lady sighs as if a mountain lay on her chest. But Severine chuckles in the bushes.

The ways of love are many. None of them led to the strange girl. None seem to have led to the lady either.

But a big, wide, well-traveled highway leads to Severine.

# *Mother*

My window faces out toward the little path. I see everyone who goes by. And everyone sees in. Some fleetingly and as if by accident, others long and curiously.

But the path curves and I can also see the nearest neighboring house. A low, white-painted country house, two-story with dormers. A garden around it with flowering cherry trees and a shiny silver ball. All of it pretty, well ordered, almost prosperous.

The pale, dark-haired boy from over there goes by. He's twelve, but looks fourteen; tall, a little round-shouldered, with a small, closed face. He walks along, then suddenly starts running. Or he bends down quickly, picks up a stone and flings it out across the field in an impulsive rush of intense resentment. Many times I've seen him with red eyes and a hard mouth, but only once with friends, laughing and talking. He never looks in; he's the only one who doesn't.

His sisters, on the other hand — they stare. They're two small girls with black hair curling over their shoulders, with thin bare legs, bare arms and bracelets. They have difficulty moving on; they walk backwards over the path, while their eyes stay glued to my window, on my newly washed white shoes that sit in the sun. On everything that can in some way help identify me, the strange city dweller. And their stares are gaping, slightly loony.

The mother comes past, a big, strong, dark woman. Her hair is a close black mass; she has gypsy eyes, a straight nose, and a clearly defined chin, in spite of her years and increasing corpulence. She has been, and still is, a devil of a woman, the sort who drives men wild. Squinting against the sun, she watches me through the window.

People say of her: smart as a whip, good-humored, easy going. Too bad she drinks so much....

For the neighbor woman does drink. Not continuously, but in bouts. At times she'll go and sit in that little room over at the general store together with Trina the Butcher and drink bock beer until she can't stand up. It goes on for several days in a row.

Then the two small girls help her home. They support her, one on each side, propping her up as best they can with the good will of children. And they look up at those they meet with little witless smiles and say, "Our mama's so sick again...."

You think they don't really understand....

I've never seen it. I hope I don't get the chance.

But the boy....

They say he can hang around for hours on the path, lying in wait alongside it in the bushes to watch out for Trina the Butcher and hinder her from coming....

They say he's fought with her. And that he follows after the two women, pleading and persuading in a low, insistent voice, taking his mother by the arm....

But when she twists away from him and goes off anyway, he runs to the woods and stays there a long time, hiding himself like a sick animal. Someone ran into him there once. His face was swollen from crying.

The days pass.

High up in the blue flutters the lark. An almost invisible pinprick in infinity, a little, quivering, exultant, tireless point that rests a couple of short, transparent night hours and eats God knows when.

The starling couple on the roof chatters away. The cat hunts butterflies. Over at the neighbor's, the garden's shiny ball glows like a sun through a cloud of white cherry blossoms, above a patterned carpet of blue-black earth, auriculas and tulips.

The dark woman washes the windows. She hangs up the laundry — good, well-kept garments in long rows. She hauls out mattresses, bolsters, pillows, comforters, lays them all over the picket fence and beats them so it echoes through the neighborhood. An efficient person, a tidy person. The children are painting the gate. The mother sets the table for coffee under the cherry trees; the bright kettle shines in competition with the silver ball. Mother and children talk to each other in high, happy voices; each one goes back to her or his task afterwards. All is peace, harmony, happy activity.

I think, people have exaggerated. They're like that....

She's expecting her husband home soon, the housewives inform me. They stand with their arms crossed over their stomachs and nod in the direction of the house over there. From whaling. Away nine months. Now three months home. Good man, you know, capable man...if he didn't sometimes drink like a fish. When it comes down to it, he's not one whit better than she is....

The tall boy's pale face looms up in my mind against a background of dark woods. And follows me a while.


One morning there's a steady traffic back and forth on the path. The three children come and go. There's shouting for the telephone and the taxi. All through the neighborhood the housewives come to their doors to look. They stand with their young ones in their arms or else with their arms crossed over their stomachs. From mouth to mouth it passes; yes, it's true, the whale-oil processing ship arrived in the night, early in the morning. The first processing ship of the year.

Now she's going to fetch him, they say, and nod in the direction of the house with the silver ball. Here she comes....

Here she comes. At full speed and all dressed up, smiling, nodding to all sides. A black straw hat with a "spray," rustically tailormade, high-heeled shoes that slow her step a little. Newly

curled and coiffed, still beautiful in spite of her age and heaviness. The men push back their caps and scratch their necks
while they stare after her. One or two of them go weak in the
knees and spit thoughtfully. She wouldn't be the worst thing
to come home to; that's the truth all right, womenfolk can say
what they want....

The taxi waits at the general store. It roars off to the
crowd's applause.

Later on in the morning it comes back. Comes all the way
up the path in spite of the taxi driver's protests. A sunburnt
man with a soft felt hat on the back of his head and a cigar in
the corner of his mouth fills the car with uproarious gaiety,
stubbornly insisting that they're going straight to the house if
he has to get out and push it from behind, and raising his hand
and his hat to everyone in their doorways. He has his arm
around his wife. She leans into him so that her spray twists
askew and laughs at everything with a deep cooing laughter
reminiscent of wild doves in the woods. The taxi is overflowing
with baggage. A stalk of green bananas on top.

Three children crowd the path and the man lifts them up
to him one after the other. Glowing with happiness at being
home again, he swings them around in a circle, so their legs are
horizontal in the air.

It's afternoon. Peaceful. Idyllic.

Happy voices have been coming from over there a long
time, punctuated by the sounds of a croquet game and the
phonograph.

The small girls pass by now and then. They drag baskets
from the general store, heavy and toilsome burdens. There's
surely nothing odd about it. A homecoming is a homecoming
...they want to have plenty.

"Bottles," mutter the housewives. "Beer bottles...."

"You can't be sure," I protest.

But they shake their heads.

Little by little it gets quiet at the neighbor's house. So no doubt they've gone in. They must be inside.


The lark pours out its larksoul without thought of economy. Everything else is quiet; the lark still keeps at it. The air vibrates with sunlight over the new spring-green meadows. Over across the yards there's not a person to be seen. It's the middle of the afternoon.

Then a shout cuts through the stillness. A shout, not terribly loud, but brimming over with fear. "Mother!" someone shouts.

It comes from the house over there.

I see the two small girls. They hang over the fence, but it's not one of them shouting, and they don't move either.

Now it comes again. It comes from inside and sounds like someone is hammering on a door. It comes again. The small girls hang as before on the palings.

It's quiet for a little while. Then the shout comes again, louder. From an open window, upstairs.

And I see the boy above the cherry tree. He is sitting in the window, holding on to the ledge, bending out as far as he can, and shouting down to the two closed windows beneath him, "Mother!"

No one answers. Nothing moves. Not even the small girls. "Mother!"

His voice breaks. A little child's sob is in the big boy's voice. "Mother!"

His shout is full of tears, of undisguised weeping. "Mother!"

And he throws himself down over the window frame with his head against it and sobs. He beats his head against the sill and wails, "Mother! Mother! Mother!"


There's nothing to be done. No hand can reach out to him

without making everything worse. The smallest gesture of sympathy is forbidden me.

The small girls continue to look into the distance with empty, rather confused faces....

An hour later the house over there resounds with voices. Above them all is hers, the mother's, raised to the highest pitch, full of the wrong kind of laughter, swinging up to a falsetto at the end of every sentence.

"No, but darling, what was it you were thinking? You thought there was something wrong with us, didn't you? What a silly boy! Come to Mother so I can kiss you! We were just resting a little. Did you ever hear the like, what *did* you think? Poor boy, getting so scared! Let me kiss you! Come on now and you can have some bananas...."

The evening is nothing but noise and good humor. The phonograph and croquet start up again. Corks pop. There are undisguised bock beer bottles on the garden table and lying empty under it. A big, strong man's booming contentment fills the garden. He swings the small girls around and around. They shriek, carried away by laughter.

After dinner the married pair strolls along the path; his eyes are glazed, she is unsteady. She hangs on his arm, looks up at him with swimming eyes. She dissolves into laughter and her voice swings up to a falsetto every other word.

Once she falls flat over the stone wall and must be helped to her feet again.

... The boy is gone.

He's run off to the woods in the twilight....

# *Larsen's*

THE COUNTRY ROAD is wide, light gray, straight as a ruler as far as the eye can see, east and west. It's well traveled. Heavy buses, reckless motorcycles, dusty Fords full of summer-clad and boisterous teenagers; now and then a soundless car of excellent make, with reserved, well-dressed passengers; now and then people on foot, barefoot youngsters with baskets on their arms.

Larsen's general store is situated by the side of the road. Whenever it hasn't rained for a couple of days everything around turns gray with dust. It lies an inch thick on the nettles at the edge of the ditch, on the lilac bushes in the garden, on the railing of the veranda, on the window sills and moldings. It forms a soft felt layer for bare young feet to shuffle in all the way up to the door, hangs like a choking cloud in the air morning to evening.

Without clearly understanding why, Mrs. Larsen loves rainy weather. As a young girl she loved sunshine. Since she married, quiet, wet weather has become a sort of release for her. It's easier to breathe and everything turns luxuriant and green. Not such a tremendous number of people go by then. The irritating feeling of having been placed here at the side of the road almost by mistake, while everyone else comes from somewhere and is going somewhere, disappears. She can open all the windows and let the breeze stream through. You don't see the dust indoors either, when there's no sun. And her legs get less tired than in sunny, warm weather.

*

The store should be closing for the day now. But young-sters with baskets on their arms are still crowding the space between the counter and the door. Mrs. Larsen reaches out and takes the baskets, while the frail hands of the children point to show that the account book is inside. She takes the empty beer bottles out and puts full ones in, writes it down in the book and gives the basket back again, good-natured and smiling, saying in a strange, gentle voice, "There you go-oh. Now it's your turn, little one...."

She bends down to the children's faces raised toward her — cheerful and shy, clean and dirty, blooming and gray as milky coffee — all mixed together. "So Papa's home again? I can see that. Well, it's good times, I can imagine. There you go-oh...."

A car stops outside. A tall boy calls in, "Larsen!"

Mrs. Larsen answers, gentle and good-natured, "Larsen's not here. He was so tired, he went to lie down; he was so late coming home last night. Was there something you needed?"

"Some gas..."

"I'm coming...."

She makes her way through the flock of children; outside she handles the gas hose — unchangingly friendly and obliging. Wonderful person, Mrs. Larsen, no nonsense. It's past closing time, but....

Then she's back in the store. "And you, little gypsy? A half pound of coffee? Three beers? There you go-oh...."

Mrs. Larsen has small, damply gleaming brown eyes, shaded by long, thick lashes. She is as downy and warm-complected as a ripe peach. Her voice is as clear as a child's, flexible, with frequent changes of key.

Mrs. Larsen is all softness and mildness and tears at the ready, tears of joy and emotion, easily aroused. A sensibility that melts over Courts-Mahler's novels and little sentimental verses in *Allers*,* that dissolves when Larsen smiles, that

---
*A popular magazine. — Trans.

reaches out blindly and longingly for tenderness and lyricism, for something Mrs. Larsen could no way express in words.

All this is thickening to a standstill behind a counter, locked inside a premature and overwhelming stoutness as inside a prison. It hungers tenaciously, among herring and laundry soap and a crabby and sleepy Larsen, after the ineffable; it won't give up the dream.

Sometimes Mrs. Larsen, in unguarded moments, when the store is empty, sags down onto a sack or barrel with a small and tired face. This often happens toward evening when the road lies darkening and quiet under a fine mist of rain, when an intense fragrance rises up from everything growing...or when the sky is gilded with red, as if intoxicated, over the tops of the trees, on the other side of all that dust, and the corncrake has begun to chirp in the field...when Mrs. Larsen should really be busy closing up, straightening, and adding up the day's receipts.

It happens now.


Ah...Larsen in a tuxedo! Larsen a little red and animated from drinking, but manly, elegant and seductive, with smooth, pomaded hair, one hand in his trouser pocket, the other holding a cigar, a silk handkerchief at his breast, a swing to his step; in an excellent mood, full of jokes, telling stories it was impossible not to laugh at, even if they were a little...were a little... well....

In short — Larsen as she'd seen him the first time. At a wedding at the Iversens'.

Larsen on the lawn in the garden later that evening, with his hat at the back of his head...a wild rose in his buttonhole ...turning to the moon, singing, "My Lord, how that moon shines..." not exactly in a resounding voice, but with a delivery, a delivery....

Larsen in the car home, aggressive, dangerous, irresistible.

Larsen during the engagement...a jaunty notions sales-man who came to visit and turned her quiet, slightly old-fashioned farm household upside down with his lively pranks, his singing; he was a breath of fresh air from the great world. He had his notion samples with him as presents for her: photograph frames, pincushions, costume jewelry, stationery and flacons of perfume...and was aggressive, dangerous and irresistible in the lilac bushes after supper....

And Larsen now!

Grumpy and peevish, in shirt sleeves and without a tie, constantly a little tousled from lying on the bed; drinking beer and smoking hour after hour with one traveling salesman or another in the living room while she watches the store; driving around late at night on "business"; hard to get up in the morning, picky about food....

Mrs. Larsen doesn't reproach him with any of this. She answers with unchanging mildness, "Yes, yes, of course," each time he explains that he unfortunately *must* go out tonight too, or that he can't manage to get up yet. Perhaps business life is like that. But she can no longer hide from herself the fact that she'd imagined wedded bliss with Larsen differently. She'd thought, for instance, that he had a more durable interest in the moon and that kind of thing than he's shown himself to have; she had believed it wasn't just on special occasions that he sang about its light. She peers and listens and continually looks for the first Larsen, the right Larsen, in all that the present Larsen says and does. Tirelessly she waits for his return. And she can't stop wishing that they'd never bought this blessed general store.

It's a disappointment as well. It wasn't, it's true, one of those just-built, naked-looking general stores that resembled a new building in the far west around which nothing had managed to grow yet. It was an old and established place. The garden was full of bushes, lilac and jasmine, currants and gooseberries. No one said a thing about the luxuriant growth having come before the road traffic became a plague or about the dust making the use of both berries and flowers impossible. The day they'd been here and inspected it, it had rained torrentially. Everything was healthy and green, cool and fragrant....

It was, of course, rather gray on the coffee table in the living room, but she'd only thought that the woman of the house wasn't really the proper type and that when she was here it would be quite different....

"Agathe!"
Mrs. Larsen jumps up, hurries across the floor and into the bedroom.

Larsen is lying on one of the unmade beds. In a state of dishevelment, in shirt sleeves and without a tie, with his vest unbuttoned. On the night table are two empty beer bottles and a glass. There are ashes in the glass and ashes and a cigar stump on the throw rug at the side of the bed. The shoes Larsen kicked off lie across the room and the chamber pot threatens to overflow.

Through the half open door, in the light of the last rays of the setting sun, Mrs. Larsen sees the dust lying an inch thick on the table and on the piano in the living room. She knows there is ash in all the flowerpots and ring marks from wet glasses here and there.

In all the rooms the air is old and closed up. There has been a whole string of sunny days and no means of opening the windows because of the traffic.

Things feel to Mrs. Larsen like they've gotten out of hand again. She always feels that way. But this wasn't at all what she dreamed of as a young girl when she thought about her future home. That was a light and airy and scrupulously neat place, a place with polished surfaces and gleaming brass, embroidered pillows and napkins, nicely and symmetrically arranged, with well-cared-for leafy plants, freshly ironed curtains, numerous framed photographs and other little things in knickknack shelves; a place full of song and music and poetry and without a speck of dust. A hunger to tackle it — to wash and scrub, rinse the flowers, take away the smudges, air everything out, first of all air everything out — comes over her every time she sets foot in her own house. Along with an unclear feeling of injustice and resentment against the store, that everlasting store.

A girl? Keep a hired girl? Larsen once said that if only they could get the upper hand of the newly established competitor at the crossroads, they'd hire a girl or some other help for the store. The competitor went bankrupt three months ago and nobody else appeared to take his place, but Larsen doesn't mention it. That he will help out, on his own initiative, is another of the things Mrs. Larsen is waiting for.

Now, however, he says in a thick, sleepy voice, "Oh, go get me a half pint of beer, please. I'm incredibly thirsty...."

Obediently she goes after one. "Do you think you'll manage to get up for supper?" she asks gently and tentatively, with only the slightest hint of tiredness and boredom in her voice. "Or will you have a bite in bed?"

"Don't know... have to see... that's my girl... ah!"

Larsen pours and drinks, empties the bottle.

He stretches himself, clears his throat and is suddenly in a good mood. "Sit here a minute, come on," he says, making a place for her on the side of the bed. "So, has it gone well today? Lots of people? Did you get an invoice on the herring? And the American lard, has it come? Hell and damnation, and the flour sack, too... that got off? That's good...."

Mrs. Larsen patiently gives an account of the day's events. She fights against a nagging loathing for everything....

Then Larsen strokes her bare arms, pulls her a little so she comes closer to him, plays with the gold heart she wears around her neck.

"Did you close up?" he asks.

And Mrs. Larsen melts. She gets tears in her eyes. Everything awful disappears into an enormous yearning, an ardent longing for the Larsen she still has hopes of winning back.

A car horn suddenly sounds outside. Many times, persistently.

"Let them honk," says Larsen.

But there's a knocking at one door, then at another. "Hmm, maybe it's best to take a look, all the same, goddammit anyway...."

Larsen goes. In person, for once. He smoothes his hair and buttons his jacket on the way, pulling his collar up to hide the fact his tie is missing. The next moment Mrs. Larsen hears glad cries and laughter out in front. A number of people are all talking at once, among them a lady.

In a complete panic she manages to set herself to rights, throws the crocheted spread over the bed, disappears via the kitchen with the full chamberpot, returns in time to see that the living room is positively crawling with people, three men and a young lady, who pour through the front door talking loudly and cheerfully.

She's dragged in and introduced. These are old friends of Larsen's, three traveling salesmen; he had a fantastically good time with them in the coast towns and on the steamers once, before he married and put down anchor here. This is the fiancée of one of the three friends, a merry young lady in city clothes, who chats and laughs and is from Bergen.

As if in a dream Mrs. Larsen hears their assurances that they wouldn't think of going past his door without looking in, now that he's got a wife and everything...wanted a look at this wife he's been hiding out here...you can't keep that up forever, ha-ha-ha...and one of them pokes Larsen in the stomach.

As if in a dream she hears him saying over and over again that now they're here they must stay and have a little supper. They wouldn't disappoint him and his wife by just going off again, would they...?

For a moment everything spins. Then she collects herself and answers that, of course not, not a bit of trouble or bother. It will be delightful....

She succeeds in getting the whole company out to the garden, seated around drinks in the summer house, while she, with the courage born of despair, hurries to wipe off the most compromising dust, slice cold cuts in the store, lay the table, fry eggs and beef and put a few pathetic curls in her hair, all at once. She has a certain thickness in her throat, but realizes that neither time nor circumstance permits tears. Bewildered, she whirls around, juggling a frying pan and a curling iron, while she relieves her distressed heart with small exclamations, like, "Oh, my... ever seen the like... this is the worst thing I've ever had happen..." Etc., etc.

Larsen comes through the door. "I'll just go in and put a tie on. No, really, we're having a great time – reliving old memories... take it easy there." She hears him in the bedroom. He pulls out drawers and shoves them in again, is there quite a while.

Then he comes back through the kitchen. "Well, I really should help you but... I can't leave them alone out there either, it would seem funny....'

She barely comprehends his words through the tremendous smoke pouring from the frying pan, much less that he has fundamentally changed his appearance in some way. It's something that surprises, pleases, and alarms her at the same time.

But she doesn't have time to think more about it; she just waves him off. "So go on out to them, then... God, now the potatoes are burning... go on, I'm almost finished."

In the back of her mind the young lady from Bergen is creating havoc. She hasn't had time to look at her but, with the help of senses other than sight, has clearly ascertained that the young lady is shapely and chic, with long, slender, high-heeled legs; powdered, red-lipped, with faultlessly arranged hair... the sort who disturbs other women.

A confident, cheerful young lady, not one bit tired or overwhelmed, one of those who is always the focal point, saying glib and amusing things... who can, however, also say something completely insignificant and still make everyone laugh and join in. Who can make you feel heavier and thicker and more shapeless than you are....

Mrs. Larsen perspires and glistens; she feels that the curls aren't going to hold out long....

But finally the moment arrives when she can cool her hands under the tap, straighten the neck of her blouse; when, dizzy with warmth and exertion, but with her voice unchangingly mild and soft, she announces, "A few sandwiches…the simplest thing… no, of course not the slightest trouble, a pleasure…please help yourself…."

When the beef has been around for the second time and she's certain there will be enough, a listless calm falls over her. She makes an effort to keep up in the conversation, laughs and answers correctly in the right places and has the leisure to take in the finer points of the Bergen lady's dress.

Each time Mrs. Larsen looks at Larsen she feels a sting of surprise. There's something about Larsen….

Suddenly, as they get up from the table and everyone clusters around to thank her for the meal, it strikes her what it is. Larsen is the way she saw him the first time; he's the way he was at the Iversens' wedding — flushed, a little animated by drink, but, masculinely elegant and seductive, not exactly in a tuxedo, but well brushed, wearing his nicest tie, with his silk handkerchief sticking up from his breast pocket and smoothly pomaded hair. The right Larsen, the lost Larsen….

In a moment, perhaps, he'll stand with one hand in his trouser pocket, the other holding a cigar, rocking on his heels….

Quite right; that's what he does…he does all of it. He's been resurrected, he's come again….

Yet Mrs. Larsen isn't proud and isn't pleased. In spite of everything she feels strangely uneasy, as if she's being duped and deceived….


Coffee is to be served in the garden. The traffic on the road has died down, the dust has died down, the crickets' chirping breaks loose, the air is full of fragrance.

"Heavens, what a wonderful evening," says the young lady from Bergen. "Aren't we having a fine time here…." She blows smoke from her cigarette in the gentlemen's faces and teaches Larsen the Charleston on the stairs….

In the kitchen Mrs. Larsen is arranging the coffee tray. She wipes the cups and sets them down, while she looks around dejectedly. Now everything is covered with dirty dishes to wash and there's a mess to clean up....

It's as if her legs grow weak under her. She has to put down the tray and use the kitchen bench to support her.

Something reaches her through all the open doors. Something she's longed for, sighed for, and yet that now strikes her like a blow. It's a song, it's notes, it's Larsen singing, "Lord, how that moon shines, see it glowing over town and country...."

And there's not even a moon at all, not a hint of a moon....

"If it had only been up," she says, offended, to no one.

She feels, for the first time, something hard and mutinous in herself, the beginnings of fury. Just as Mrs. Larsen comes out on the steps with the coffee tray, the young lady from Bergen cries, "Da capo!" And the others chime in, "Da capo, da capo...."

Larsen is on the second round of "see it glowing" when Mrs. Larsen sets the tray on the summer house table and makes a pointed and uncalled-for rattling. She doesn't wait until he's finished but pours the coffee immediately and offers it around in a loud voice. "A cup of coffee, here you are."

She feels how the others exchange outraged looks among themselves, thinking, My God, what kind of a wife does he have — poor Larsen!

She feels pain and malicious pleasure and a kind of inexplicable compassion for Larsen, because he lives with her behind a boring general store, instead of constantly singing — manly, elegant and seductive — for fine, new young ladies from other places... she feels anguish and defiance... all at the same time.

Two round and lonely tears, hidden by the twilight, glide slowly down over her cheeks. They've been waiting a long time, since before supper, in the kitchen. Tears of a new and bitter blend...

That resemble none of the many Mrs. Larsen has shed before in her life.

# *Bernhardt*

He walks around the house. Around and around on the little path he himself has worn down, the summer path. Once again edged with all sorts of lush growth, it's dry and firm, easy to walk on.

Now and then he stops, cocks his head and listens. Or he bends down and fingers something, touching it quickly and carefully, as if eager not to hurt it.

It can be the big tuft of grass that bristles above everything else in one corner; the obstinate scufflers that hold their own here and there on the path even though he's always trudging over them; the wild pansies over on the south wall. Warmth rises up toward him from everything, genial and comforting. Every time he rounds a corner there is something familiar, growing and waiting. He recognizes the grass' way of springing up.

His tall stooped body with the awkwardly long, shuffling legs moves at a steady tempo alongside the white house. On the south and west wall, a ludicrous shadow follows him.

Just above his head, around him and the house and the small garden's slope, rests a cloud, an overstuffed comforter of apple blossoms. The air is saturated with fragrance and with buzzing.

"He's happy now, that Bernhardt, poor devil," say the neighbor women. They pause a little on the path between the kitchen and the shed and peer at him under the branches. "That's no small cross Josefine has to bear, and that's the truth..." They sigh, troubled, for they have their crosses too. Everyone does, no one can escape. But you have to admit that Josefine has something especially pitiful in Bernhardt.

In Bernhardt's face the mouth is almost rectangular. This is because it always hangs open and is bordered on each side by a long yellow eyetooth, all that's left of his front teeth. His eyes are blue, soft, trustful. Sometimes a sort of shadow passes across them...but since he can't say a word there's no one who knows what that means. Where Bernhardt lives, the importance of speech is as good as absolute. Shadows across the eyes are nothing to pay much attention to.

His mother comes out on the steps and looks around. Bernhardt is, at the moment, on the other side. She stamps her foot a little, the way you do when you want to scare an animal away...and Bernhardt hastens forward. That's his signal, the one he's always listening for.

"The pail, Bernhardt," says his mother, and hands him the garbage pail. Bernhardt nods, understanding and eager; he grips the pail and strides off with it behind the wall of the shed, as businesslike as one entrusted with a great task.

Then he starts walking around the house again. And look, every time he swings around one corner, there's the tuft of grass bristling, and every time he comes around the other, the pansies turn their delicate, wondering faces up toward him. But giants are what they are, and they don't allow anyone to get the upper hand of them. And it was like that yesterday and the day before yesterday, last year and the year before that, back through a chain of summers and days, right from the moment Bernhardt began his groping and shuffling way here on earth. It's just as new and remarkable and joyful this time as it always was. That is Bernhardt's experience.

There's a tramping on the steps again and he speeds up.

"The hens, Bernhardt," his mother says and hands him a peeling enamel dish with leftovers in it. He nods wisely and sets off for the hen house, balancing the dish with both hands, far away from him. He's in Sunday dress today, Bernhardt, in black clothes. He has on a tie and a collar and a stiff hat; he doesn't want to get dirty in any way. His mother watches him and wags her head, smiling, touched by the care with which he treats his clothes. "He's a good boy," she mumbles, appreciating his better sides. "The good thing about him is how nice he is."

She goes in again.

Just as Bernhardt is on the way to the hen house someone suddenly hails him from the garden gate.

"Oh, excuse me, is this the way...?" calls a voice and says the name of a farm.

Bernhardt simply goes on without turning his head. Everyone knows that he can't tell the way, whether here or there. Those who don't know, you have to watch out for. Bernhardt learned that the other day; he turned his head to look at who was speaking.

But the voice calls again and louder, as if it's talking to a deaf person. It's a clear voice and doesn't seem dangerous. He understands that something out of the ordinary is happening and turns his face with its rectangular mouth toward the gate.

"Oh," says the voice apologetically, half to itself.

For a moment Bernhardt remains standing and looking. Something half-forgotten, an old memory from last year and from the years before flickers up inside. He's seen such things before. They usually ask the way and have their hands full of flowers, just like this. They're never dangerous, don't get angry, are more often afraid of him and run away. They're called city ladies. When they begin to turn up, it's definitely summer.

He continues on his way. He has a task, is focused on it, is on his way toward it. Besides, there's nothing he can do in this case.

The city lady leans on the gate. She's red and warm from having gone too far and too fast, bareheaded, without protection against the sun. Her bare arms and her chest above the low neckline of her dress seem lit from the inside by too sudden and too strong a sunburn. She's lost her way, poor city lady, has walked and walked on hot dry roads without shade, and she can hardly take any more. She makes up her mind and opens the gate, climbs the stairs and knocks on the door.

Josefine looms, tall and bent, bland and obliging in her net of wrinkles. Yes, this is certainly the right road. All you have to do is keep going and stick to the right. She takes the city lady's arm cautiously. "Tell me, you weren't afraid of him, the one who just walked across the yard, were you?"

"No, I wasn't," says the city woman. "I understood that he was deaf," she adds, considerately. Deaf, that's always a little less brutal than idiot.

"Not deaf," exclaims Josefine, becoming animated. "Not deaf. Deaf he's not. Hears just as good as you and me. I should say! No, I'll tell you what's wrong with him...he can't say a word." Josefine's voice sinks to the level of a confidential communication. "It's nerves, the doctor says...the nerves here..." She touches herself by way of explanation on the throat and strokes it. "Meningitis, dear! When he was six months old. But the doctor says there's nothing wrong with him except he can't talk."

Bernhardt has meanwhile returned, his mission carried out. He's set the empty dish down and is cautiously approaching.

"No, but you weren't afraid of him," continues Josefine, and is happy about this fact. "I'll tell you this, someone was here the other day, a man driving by in a car, who asked the way too, and poor Bernhardt just stood there and gaped. Then the other guy got so mad he was close to hitting him. 'I'll teach you, you fool, to stand there staring at people with your mouth open, not answering,' he shouted. And Bernhardt, he got so afraid after that he ran inside and hid himself."

"I can't understand that," says the city lady.

"No, you can hardly believe somebody being so angry! You can see right away that this poor boy isn't exactly like other people. Yes, you saw that all right, dear...."

"I'll tell you this," confides Josefine, and gets even closer and becomes even more familiar. "I'll tell you this, that he's

such a good boy. He just trudges along, helping with one thing
and another. I can just say to him — Bernhardt, I say — and right
away he understands. Because he really does understand some
things, you see, even though he can't talk. I should say! And
he walks around the house, too, dear. Here, look, he's tramped
that path way down by himself. He's walked and walked here
summer after summer ever since he was a little boy, and he'll
be twenty-three come fall. I don't dare let him out in the road,
you see, because of the cars...."

The city lady regards the path intently, moved, but she's
not able to say anything, for Josefine has warmed to her subject.
"But isn't it wonderful, dear, how nice he is? Yes, I say you
can't be thankful enough for that, because this way I can have
him at home. I've seen enough of that, I can tell you, how it is
for them who are taken away. He's just like a child, you understand. Has to be helped with everything, exactly like a little
child. He can't help himself with anything. I've got to mash up
his food for him like you do for a baby, because he doesn't have
any teeth, you see. It's all the medicine he's gotten, that's
what's destroyed his teeth."

Bernhardt stands behind the city lady. Shadows cross his
eyes.

"But I'm so glad I can have him home," Josefine says again.

"I understand that," says the city lady.

She's lightly clad and her hair sits like a little narrow and
glimmering silk skullcap down over her ears, short, shiny and
nutbrown. It reminds Bernhardt of something he's seen before,
what can it be? Of course, now he has it. What the storekeeper's
wife wears on Sunday, that shines so brightly around her thick
arms...what Josefine and the housewives call silk sweaters.
Mrs. Larsen's silk sweater.

He can't help himself, he has to reach for this soft, glisten-
ing stuff that is so different from the dry wisps on Josefine's and
the housewives' heads...feel it. This is, after all, Bernhardt's
way of experiencing.

He reaches.

The city lady starts, but immediately recovers and smiles

at him and Josefine, who assures her, "He's a good boy, really, he doesn't mean any harm, he just has to touch everything he thinks is pretty...."

The city lady may be neither young nor pretty. At least nothing special when it comes to city ladies. But everything is relative. Next to Josefine she's a revelation...straight posture, short skirt, bright from head to toe, right down to her shoes. The longer she stands there, the more Bernhardt realizes that city ladies are most interesting to him at close range. Never before has he beheld one of them so long and so uninterruptedly. No one has come through the gate before; many were afraid and ran from the sight of him.

There's something delightful about them. You'd like to touch them everywhere....

Bernhardt touches her hair again. The city lady smiles once more, a little nervously. She acts like she wants to go and says, "Thanks very much, now I can find my way...."

Bernhardt is looking at a bare arm, so different again from Josefine's dry, yellowish-brown sticks.

He stretches his hand out and touches it. At the same time a remarkable sound works its way up from his breast; he's capable of bringing it out now and then for big events.

The city lady is startled. She turns. And opens her eyes wide in horror.

For she's looking right into something she doesn't dare acknowledge in a face like this.

It's pouring out of the helpless features. An agitation, blind and shackled, directed as if by some natural force, wind or waves. With no will of its own to seek out, find and take what it wants....

The city lady quickly takes a couple of steps. But she's no cruel or completely insensitive city lady. Through her horror and aversion she feels a painful sting of pity. She does something laughable. She turns around and, with a little, confused, "Here you are," she fills Bernhardt's arms with all her flowers and rushes down to the gate and out to the country road.

He stands there with his arms full as a prima donna's.

There are avens and wild chervil, buttercups and sorrel, things only a city lady would think to pick. He gapes more than ever.

Down by the gate Josefine calls, "He's not dangerous, dear. I can guarantee you that...you needn't be afraid...he's really such a good boy...."

# Shit-Katrine

THERE'S A FACE I can't shake off, one of the faces from my childhood. Suddenly and unexpectedly it breaks free of memory's chaos to look at me. With a backdrop of wharves and alleys, of everything that was gloomy and furtive in a little town in Finnmark.

A dark shawl covers half of it, concealing the forehead and mouth, hiding the hair, half the body and half a heavy basket carried on one arm. Shifting, flickering shadows from the fading winter's day and the newly lit street lamps fall over it, giving it a free-floating, undefined shape.

Or I see it bare, with the shawl back around the neck, exposed to the summer's incessant light. The hair hangs in unkempt tangles around it. The upper lip lifts in a slow-witted leer over a few teeth. The skin has that thick grayness that comes from neglect and poverty. Around the throat, on a black velvet band, a little medallion.

It's Katrine, Shit-Katrine, the lowest, most wretched of us all in that little community there at home – she who we called, without hedging, the whore. A brick in the wall, she too, a pitiful brick that in turn held up others, an institution... and at the same time, the town's shame and disgrace, the scapegoat, who no one wanted to acknowledge, who no one saw.

She wasn't the only one, far from it. There was, for example, Peg-Leg Fina. She was no different and no better than

Katrine and you could hardly say she enjoyed respect. But she knew how to assert herself, in spite of her position; she was neither shouted after nor called names when she came clumping through the street, a large, robust person, red-cheeked and golden-haired, with a certain air of neatness about her. Peg-Leg Fina wore a clean shirtwaist under her shawl and her hair was slicked with water into a top-knot and curled bangs. She didn't lug around a basket and make as if she were out on another errand than she was, but acknowledged the facts and looked people in the eye, put her hands on her hips and spoke up when necessary; her tongue was feared. That's an asset in this world.

And then there were two sisters who always walked together. They were no beauties, were fat and aging. But there were two of them; they could laugh and be cheerful, with their slicked-back hair and curled bangs. Each of them even wore a long, gold watch chain over her breast when they went coatless in summer. There were, to be sure, those who said there was nothing but gold-brass in the chains, but all the same...both Fina and the sisters were far superior to Katrine. We won't even mention Palmine Flor and Lilly Vogel. They wore hats. They wore boas in the winter and studs in their ears. There's an abyss just between shawls and hats.

Katrine—she was the way she was, unkempt and toothless. Whatever she wore under her shawl certainly couldn't be given the name of a piece of clothing. It was as gray, shabby and faded as she was; something without color or shape held together by pins. She didn't walk down the middle of the street as if there were nothing to be ashamed of, but stole along the quays and concealed herself in alleys, dragging her basket along so it pulled her crookedly to one side—there was no telling what she had in it. She might also be carrying a string of fish or a birch-bark basket; still, she never loitered openly.

She had no natural gifts, not even for brashness. That's why her life was the way it was...all the contempt the others avoided was dumped on her. She might have a whole gang of boys shouting and calling after her and there would be the children of the better-off folk, the ones you'd least expect it from, among them. Heckling Katrine was no mean entertainment on a long and aimless afternoon...you could count on the result. She would walk a while without answering, her face red and hard. Then she wouldn't be able to contain herself. She'd turn to her pursuers, stutter and stammer in her search for something to sling back at them, something powerful and incisive. Each time she would find only one word. "Shit," she cried. "Shit and shit and shit!"

Many people get nicknames in a small town. That hers became Shit-Katrine goes without saying.

I remember her middle-aged and tragic, hurrying along with boys after her.

I remember her when she, in the twilight and in secluded spots, was out with her seductive wiles, tarrying along the way, lifting her shawl from her face, simpering and raising an eyebrow as the custom was. To see Katrine strike up a conversation with someone, perhaps be put aboard a boat, made us thrill and shudder. We plucked each other on the coatsleeves, excited and shocked. For no one was as sinful as Katrine; no one had fallen and sunk so low as she had.

I remember her a little drunk and terribly disheveled, being led away by policeman Olsen, doing his duty. It was no joke when policeman Olsen did his duty. His face was a knot of pale seriousness, the eyes taut with energy; even the gold on his cap increased in brightness and meaning.

Katrine babbled, repeating herself and explaining; she made small, comic efforts to tear herself loose. But Olsen had managed more difficult prisoners than she. Without answering, he steered a course right for the courthouse and arrest. Around them the street was thick with people who trotted along in the same direction. Katrine's arrest was an event on par with a lesser fire or an eviction in front of a jeering crowd.

At the courthouse steps arose a crowding and confusion, because some of the pushier elements stormed up the steps and wanted to follow her inside. In the midst of it all Katrine broke free for an instant, turned and called out to Palmine Flor and Lilly Vogel, who were among the crowd gathered, that they thought they were so swell now because they wore hats....

Then she was pulled backwards through the door and disappeared from our view.

I see her on that unfortunate day in church.

You may well ask what Katrine thought she was doing there, and maintain that surely it was the one place she shouldn't have come. But who among us hasn't committed some sort of grand folly or other in our life?

It was the day that Pastor Pio was going to preach for the first time, and it was full to the last seat. There was also a new parish clerk that day, an out-of-town man, inspired by the zeal and fervor of the novice. He was busy seating people. Beckoning, counting, nodding, he persuaded and brought them to their seats. An order-loving parish clerk. The sight of people standing was an intolerable eyesore to him. Not until far into the second hymn had he gotten things under control with the latecomers.

The service was underway. Then something of a stir went through the pews and the singing grew confused. Up through the aisle came the parish clerk with yet another person, one he must have had to go all the way to the door to fetch. That person was Katrine, in a hat and jacket, two poor, ridiculous, faded garments that had probably once served as her confirmation attire. She didn't exactly go willingly; she resisted so much that her hat tilted over one ear. But there are limits to the resistance you can put up in church – outright struggling isn't done. The parish clerk kept his grip and the pair advanced quickly. Tailor Kvandal, who saw that it was building up to a scandal and was a tactful man...he'd often had occasion to show it...got up from his seat in the center of the church...where he belonged...and waved and pointed to show there was room here; he was willing to sacrifice himself and avert catastrophe. But the new parish clerk shook his head with raised brows. He made a calming sign with his hand for Tailor Kvandal to just sit down again, and continued up the aisle, happily ignorant of what he was really doing. In defiance of all unwritten caste laws Katrine was finally squeezed into the only empty seat there was, between Miss Liberg and old Consul Stoppenbrink, right under the pulpit and facing the congregation. The parish clerk gave her a last shove to make sure she was well in, because Miss Liberg made herself wider and pretended that the bench was fully occupied. But he showed her and the congregation that he knew how many could reasonably sit there and also that there was no difference between high and low for him in the Lord's house. He retreated with the discreet unctuousness to which a first-class conscience is entitled.

Miss Liberg took it wonderfully, it was generally acknowledged. For she didn't get up and leave, as many might have done in her place. She simply turned away during the rest of the service, as well as she could. That she was extremely upset was very obvious.

As for old Stoppenbrink, he was really a phenomenon, completely remarkable for his age. But everyone knew he no longer always recognized those nearest to him. Therefore, no one was surprised that he didn't recognize Katrine. He greeted her politely and moved a little to give her more room. He kept singing, following with his finger in the hymn book.

There sat Katrine, red as a turkey, trying to get her hat back on straight. She gave it a series of small, bewildered shoves and nudges that missed the mark and for some time only resulted in making it lurch in the opposite direction. Her gaze wandered, then buried itself in the hymn book she opened up, totally at random. It later turned out, as was confirmed by many who sat in the first row right below, that, to begin with, she'd held the book upside down and that it had been shaking enough to be observed far away.

Down through the rows elbow nudged elbow. Faces turned quietly to each other and exchanged glances. Katrine appeared to be distracting the congregation considerably.

When the singing died down, she continued to keep her

eyes on the floor, not looking up. But old Stoppenbrink, who up to now had been receiving discreet and sympathetic assistance from Miss Liberg, at this moment turned, to the general consternation, to Katrine and shouted into her ear...so you could hear it all over church, "My dear young lady, will you be so kind as to tell me which number we are going to sing now. ...Let me tell you, I don't see so well...."

Katrine didn't understand. She gave a start on the bench, sat and gaped. A little wave of hilarity, held back with difficulty, passed through the rows. And old Stoppenbrink shouted once again, making it all shorter and clearer, "The hymn number, young lady, the number of the hymn. Lately my sight has been getting weaker..."

Miss Liberg, averting catastrophe, leaned over, "374, Consul...374..."

"I can't hear," shouted the consul. "I didn't catch it...my hearing isn't so good either, unfortunately..."

"374," came suddenly, loud and defiant, from Katrine; she looked straight at the congregation as she spoke. Then she lowered her gaze again. But old Stoppenbrink extended his hymn book to her with an endearing old man's smile. "Then you can perhaps do an old gentleman the service of finding the hymn for me...I tell you, my sight...."

And while the singing swelled up again and took everyone in its sheltering embrace, Katrine, with fumbling fingers, found 374 for old Stoppenbrink and gave it back to him, pointing.

The next time Miss Liberg leaned forward and cried, "201, Consul." She formed the words plainly with her lips as you do for the deaf. At the same time she said in a quick and muffled, but audible, voice to Katrine, "It's best if you change places with me...."

But Katrine pretended not to hear. And shouted on her own, "201."

Old Stoppenbrink understood, smiled gratefully and handed her his hymn book. Katrine opened it and pointed, and her face was hard and strange. She made a callous and repellant impression on us all.

But during the sermon she collapsed with a bowed head and lowered eyes. Her redness disappeared little by little; in its place came a sickly paleness. When old Stoppenbrink once again turned to her, for the final hymn, this time with only a smile of request, for he now plainly found their mutual understanding such that words were superfluous, Miss Liberg moved in unhindered and straightened things out. Katrine was defeated.

At last it was over. While the organ played the last dying, disorderly tones, people streamed slowly out of the church. There was excitement in the air, an impatience to get outside and trade observations. Out of respect for the holy place you didn't go beyond an elbow nudge, a small, quick smile, and a quietly exchanged glance. One or two turned around and craned their necks, but they were people without any sense of what was proper.

Then the stream stopped. For old Stoppenbrink shouted once again. And now people lost all shame; they stopped and stood on tiptoe.

"Tell me who you are, you who've been so helpful toward an old gentleman like me?" shouted old Stoppenbrink.

I believe everyone looked around. And it was no small fraction of the town's eyes Katrine had on her when she answered in a half-choked voice, "Katrine Hansen."

"Who? I didn't hear."

"Katrine Hansen."

"A little louder, please. I tell you, my hearing…"

"Katrine Hansen," Katrine shouted, tremendously loud. Something wild came into her eyes. Those who were near her stepped back a little....

"Hansen? You said Hansen? You couldn't be by any chance the daughter of my old friend Julius Hansen...."

But Katrine suddenly bolted, as if she wanted to charge right over us. Tears ran, round and clear, down her heated face.

A way opened for her as if by itself. People pulled each other away. Old Stoppenbrink shouted wonderingly, "Tell me, did the lady leave?"

Certainly there were many of us who at that moment felt
secretly sorry for Katrine. But you have to be careful not to be
one of those who encourages vice...so no one said anything
along those lines. On the other hand, Miss Liberg won general
approval when, outside church, to a large circle, as if addressing
the entire world, she raised her voice and asked loudly, "Can
you tell me what that kind of person is doing in a church, now
really?"

No one could. And that was a relief....

Clearest of all I remember Katrine in the sorrowful twilight one misty, thawing day during the arctic night. One of
those days when so much black and gray appears in the landscape that the snow shines more sharply because of it, seeming
to emit its own light, eerie and dead.

It was out at Oset near her dwelling, a crooked, tiny little
house. She was exchanging words with a man from one of the
coalships, a somewhat drunken man who spoke in the Trøn-
delag dialect.

The conversation between them was strangely enthrall-
ing. It unfolded with splendor and brilliance, becoming like a
sparkling rift in the colorless day. And the splendor had something bargain-basement and forbidden about it, something
cheap and depraved that added to the excitement. The boys
who stood around listening had a faraway look in their eyes as
if they were being initiated into something. For once no one
was making fun.

"That's just rubbish," said Katrine.

"Ain't rubbish," said the man. "It ain't rubbish. You can
ask anyone you want who's been down there."

"They don't go round wearing silk," said Katrine.

"They go round in silk, sure," said the man. "And in gold,
and jewels and veils and fine things...."

"Not in silk," said Katrine, low and firm, addressing herself more to the rest of the world than to this unreasonable man.
The question of silk seemed important to her.

Now the man was heckling her; he closed in on Katrine. Maybe she thought girls there was like girls here. 'Cause they weren't. They were finer than the bigwigs' girls here, than the governor's girls and than the consul's girls....

"Hah," said Katrine.

Then the man closed in on her even more. So they weren't, were they? So they didn't have their own street where only them lived? Didn't they sit in front of their doors in finery the whole day? Wasn't there parties and balls every single evening up and down the whole street, wasn't there music and wine and fine liquors at their places, the whole lot of them? He was just asking....

Katrine became meek and thoughtful. She didn't argue anymore, just mumbled a couple of times, "You shouldn't go around talking lies."

But he wasn't talking lies. He even endowed the mysterious beings he spoke of with more festive qualities. Couldn't they dance? Didn't they have flowers in their hair? Weren't their faces painted? Did Katrine think they looked like her? 'Cause they didn't.

"They don't go around in silk though," said Katrine one more time, but feebly and listlessly, without conviction.

The man had gained control. With his hands in his trouser pockets he spoke uncontradicted; he started to leave and turned around again to say a little more and to secure his victory.

Unfortunately he couldn't quite keep on his subject any longer. He got mixed up in things without any interest, touched on bigwigs in general and on the harbor master in particular, mentioning the lighting conditions at the harbor. He was actually on his way into town, had already taken a few steps when Katrine suddenly became completely furious. She clenched her fists, shook them helplessly and shouted loudly, "Shit, shit, shit," so that it paralyzed her throat. It was plainly addressed to all of us, to the whole universe. And she pulled her shawl around her shoulders, turned and went, gray in all that gray. Back toward the little gray house. We heard her mumble to herself.

It was almost completely dark and the sea began to roar. It turned nasty that night. We children went home, full of wonder and an inexplicable uneasiness.


This face from my childhood haunts me. It suddenly breaks free of memory's chaos and looks at me. It torments me. It accuses me.

# *Klara*

"You be quiet now, Schjelderup, honey. You be careful now when you go out! And *thanks* for the nice evening!"

Klara is whispering this, wearing only a slip and with her arms around the neck of a man hidden in shadow. He has on a visored cap but otherwise his clothes are disheveled; he's impatiently putting himself to rights, getting ready to leave her.

Tender and tousled she clings to him; her eyes, mouth, hands won't let him go. She keeps kissing and hugging and squeezing and saying the same thing over and over again. In the meantime he buttons his vest, unmoved and purposeful, puts on his cuffs and his watch and straightens his tie, as well as he's able, with Klara hanging all over him and without a mirror. There's one over the bureau but it doesn't catch the light and he's in a hurry.

"Thank *you*," he says. "Thank you. Oh, goddammit, a button's popped off. All right, now all I have to do is get away without the old biddy hearing. Good-night, Klara!"

"Do you love me?" Klara whispers. "Do you really love me? Say it, Schjelderup, *say* you love me!"

They move over to the window together. Schjelderup opens it and slings a leg over the sill. "Yes, yes, yes, of course I do. Klara, you know that. Ouch, those damned roses! Why do people have things like that on their walls? They stick like hell...."

He sits astride the window sill for an instant, still entwined with Klara, who continues to whisper, "Yes, because I *love* you, you know. God, how I *love* you, Schjelderup."

Schjelderup slings his other leg over the sill. He turns his
head this way and that and listens, all too obviously, to something other than Klara.

"Psst, hey Klara, thanks for a nice evening," he then says
resolutely, detaching her arms from his shoulders, taking hold
of the transom and letting himself glide down along the wall
outside. He curses once again, low and fervently, over the
climbing roses and lands with a thump in the heavy spring soil
of the flower border. For a moment he stands there shifting his
feet back and forth, knocking the clumps of earth from his
shoes while Klara hangs a breakneck distance out the window
and stagewhispers, "Oh, how I love you, Schjelderup. I've
never loved anyone like you...."

"Hush up, are you crazy? They can hear you, girl."

"You'll be at the dance again on Saturday?"

"Sure I will, sure."

He puts his hand to his cap and salutes her, then moves
off into the cloudy, spicy May night, becoming a vague shadow,
disappearing....

Klara lingers at the open window until she hears that he's
over the picket fence; then she gets up, stretches and yawns.
The night air pours in, stingingly fresh, and breaks up the
closed atmosphere of cheap cigar, perfume, beer and bodies.

She walks around a little, barefoot, the strap of her slip
falling over one shoulder. With apparent absent-mindedness
she lets an empty beer bottle accidentally disappear into the
darkness between the bureau and the wall; she brushes cigar
ashes from the night table into the hollow of her hand and
throws them out, gives the pile of dirty clothes under the bed
a kick and then another, so it's pushed far underneath. She
sighs happily a couple of times.

A small table lamp illuminates the room's interior with a
weak, rose-red glow and makes the dawn light outside blue.
The first little lonely bird chirp is heard from the garden, then
it's still again.

Over the back of a chair hangs Klara's party outfit, a thin,
wrinkled rag of a voile dress with something that was once a

big green poppy at the hip. She stops and plucks at the poppy, gives it, with her scrubby red and all-too-plump hand, a number of small, invigorating pokes, imitating a saleswoman in a fashion store, prinking with her little finger extended.

Then she gives up on the poppy, yawns again, closes the window, and shakes up the pillow; she's about to go to bed, but she stops, struck by a thought.

"What was his name, I wonder. I mean, besides Schjelderup? Was it Olsen? I've completely forgotten it, haven't I? I'm really impossible."

Just as Klara, in bitter self-knowledge, is mumbling this and at the same time setting the alarm clock, something happens that, of all things, wasn't meant to happen. The door opens. The merchant's wife stands on the threshold in a violet dressing gown, with her hair full of curlers.

Klara stares at her, alarmed, pulling her slip up around her.

"Klara," says Mrs. Hjort, "it smells of cigar in here. I can smell it all the way up in my bedroom."

"It smells of what?" Klara looks perplexed for an instant, but collects herself with amazing speed, as if it weren't the first time the lady of the house had stood in the doorway in the middle of the night, saying that it smelled of cigar. "It must be from the merchant then."

"It's *not* from the merchant. He smokes different cigars. It's from tonight and from down here. Do you smoke yourself, perhaps?"

"Sometimes."

"Cigars?"

"It's all the same, I suppose," Klara retorts. "As a matter of fact I do have a cigar now and then."

"I see. One of the beer bottles is gone again. We had twelve delivered yesterday afternoon. Now there are only eleven."

"Well, it must have been the merchant. It couldn't have been anyone else."

"It's not the merchant." Mrs. Hjort casts a searching look around the room but, discovering no beer bottle, goes resolutely over to smell the glass on the night table. "Do you still maintain that it's the merchant?" she asks coldly.

"A person can certainly get the urge for a glass of beer now and then."

"Naturally. Especially after a cigar. However, you know very well what I mean, Klara. It's not the first time I've gotten up from my comfortable bed to see what was going on here. The open air dance stops at twelve o'clock. It's a ten-minute walk and I heard you come in."

"Well, all right then," answers Klara hopefully and with a little disdain in her voice as if her alibi were so obvious now that it no longer needed discussion.

But Mrs. Hjort perseveres, "Can you tell me why you're up at this time of night? It's almost three o'clock."

"I'm not up...I...I got up to turn the alarm on," says Klara. She's still holding the clock in her hand, and she holds it out to Mrs. Hjort as additional proof.

"Then you could have turned off the light while you were at it, I think. It's not really necessary to have it on, it's almost daylight." Mrs. Hjort goes over and turns off the light. The pale dawn fills the room and pitilessly lays bare the faces of the two women: Mrs. Hjort's tired, middle-aged, and Klara's colorless, exhausted.

"I've told you before, Klara, if you have a boyfriend he can come and visit you now and then in the evening, and you can certainly invite him in for a glass of beer. But male visitors at night is something we can't allow. I tell you this for your own good."

"There are no males visiting around here at night."

"One jumped over the fence a minute ago."

"Over the fence?" Klara blinks quickly a couple of times, momentarily struck dumb. But she recovers. The situation isn't new for her at all; she just needs a minute to think. "I can't help it if people jump over the fence at night...I can't help it...."

Mrs. Hjort's face grows hard under the curlers. She lets the subject drop, but takes up another instead.

"The way it looks around here," she says. "What do you

have there under the bed? Is it clothes? Dirty linen? Ugh! And what a smell in here. Smells just like a pigsty. I don't like your girlfriends either. That Konstance – it's quite possible she's a good girl, but she looks disgusting anyway. I'd hoped you'd become friends with the girls at the doctor's – they're fine, lovely girls, but no. I took you on, even though you didn't have any proper references, because you looked nice, but I can see that I made a mistake there too. You can stay until the first, but then you'll have to move. Good-night, Klara."

Without pausing Mrs. Hjort has unburdened her heart at full speed. Now it's done and now she goes. She's almost out the door before Klara finds a reply. But then she finds one that isn't inappropriate. "I'm going to get married anyway, so it doesn't matter," she calls.

"Well, then it works out just fine," answers Mrs. Hjort, keeping her dignity and closing the door after her. The shuffling step of her slippers is heard on the stairs and disappears.

Klara makes a face at the closed door. Once. Twice. Then she breaks into tears, snuffling as helplessly as a child who's gotten a scolding.

"Can I help it? Just as if I could help it!" she hiccoughs as she pulls the bedcovers over her. "They don't care about you if you don't. They just go find someone else. You see that all the time. If I could only understand why it's supposed to be so awful. Married ladies themselves...."

Here Klara's reflections stop. There are problems that are unsolvable. Wives are wives. Married. It's as undeniable as it can be. If only Klara were, too. She longs for nothing else.

The bed is still warm down under the covers. Klara's crying subsides like a child's, safe in a comforting lap. She yawns. "Schjelderup, honey," she mumbles. "You're my baby. You won't leave me, will you? You're not like that, the kind who runs away. You're not, are you? No, you're not...."

Klara yawns again. Then she sleeps.

There's nothing hard or brash about Klara. She's just

created a defense system for herself that primarily consists of ignoring facts. But how else can anyone make it through this difficult life?

She's a little too fat with a big pink mouth and damp blue eyes in a pale white face.

No man mistakes what Klara is; they target her right away. They either don't care about her at all, or their eyes light up with a cheerful little glint as soon as they see her. They sense weakness. There's something of that, too, in Klara's walk; one foot is pigeon-toed.

They whistle to her in passing. They turn and walk after her, wait for her in doorways and dark stairwells, whisper to her, take hold of her, are from the very outset bold and aggressive.

A victim, easy for them to capture, easy to throw away again with a shrug of the shoulders, a "She was so willing, really. She came on her own, she's like that...."

One predestined to be exploited by them, despised by them, debased by them — that's Klara.

There's been a shop attendant in Klara's life. A house painter. A chimney sweep. A couple of nondescript types from the open air dances. Just no one who was serious, no one who didn't drift away again. One time she was relieved of her bankbook, another time she had a baby she had to take home to her parents. She's been firmly forbidden to bring home another. Klara cries at times, is dejected and melancholy. Until she's waited for, held and kissed and whispered to by a new representative. For love, as well as faith and hope, live on in Klara's mind.

Klara has had a good position here, in a villa, working for a merchant. It's been up and down that way. Here she's had a pretty room overlooking the garden. She's also had places where she had to sleep in a cubbyhole or in the kitchen. That was how she got into the habit of kicking her possessions under the bed. You have to put your things somewhere. And then one fine night the wife of the house might stand in the kitchen door, sniffing around, saying, "It smells of cigar in here. Someone's been taking the beer bottles again. This won't do. You'll have to leave."

"You'll have to leave" – these words are like a little theme in Klara's life, constantly popping up anew. The leitmotif, so to speak.

Now she'll have to go off again with her bureau and her wicker trunk, her painful, high-heeled, worn-down shoes, her impractical hat of transparent silk straw, with its cluster of flowers under the brim near her ear. Mrs. Hjort hasn't said anything about trying a bit longer or anything like that. On the contrary, she has, in a slightly peculiar tone, expressed her happiness that Klara is going to be married, and her hope that it will be to a good man. Klara has hastily found herself a situation with a photographer in a back street of the city.

She'll have to sleep in the studio there, behind the screen used as a backdrop for photographs. It's no use being fussy about it – it's just going to be temporary, isn't it? Klara can't imagine anything else. Maybe she won't go to the photographer's at all, if she can only meet Schjelderup and talk with him. If she remembers correctly, he has work at the moment; he did mention something about it. Once again Klara sees the glimmer of bright possibilities: security and a shiny ring on her finger; her child brought from home, toddling around her skirts; gainful employment in her own kitchen.

She hums over her work. In spite of the photographer in the back street, in spite of everything. Until she suddenly comes to think about deceit and falseness and everything she's been through. Then she dries the corners of her eyes quickly with the back of her hand and rubs harder at what she's holding.

For truly, you can't be anything but sorry for Mrs. Hjort, even though she is married. Every day except Sunday she disappears upstairs at four-thirty. When she comes down again she's changed her dress and pinned the little false curls from Paris in her hair, around her temples. The train from town whistles and Mrs. Hjort goes to the gate, standing there dressed up and ready, straightening her cuffs and waiting for the merchant. And the merchant, who can't walk very fast because of a handicap, comes slowly into view around the bend.

He somehow doesn't see Mrs. Hjort, though she holds up her hand and even waves. But there's nothing wrong with his sight, for if he has friends who've come out with him or is in someone's company he waves back.

At the table it's only the missus who says anything. The merchant chews, stops now and then to pronounce a short yes or no, feels his pulse from time to time and says hmm, hmm, and chews some more. Afterwards there's the newspaper and the radio and tea at eight o'clock and solitaire and the radio again, if there's no deskwork. Not many words are exchanged. Mrs. Hjort sits there, refined and diligent, while her cheeks and the corners of her mouth droop more and more over her embroidery. At the stroke of ten each of them goes to his or her room.

Yes, well, she's old, poor thing. Men are all alike, even if they're over sixty like the merchant. She's a pretty easy going missus in many ways – Klara can't deny it – just unreasonably picky. And she's definitely like other missuses when it comes to having men friends in your room at night now and then. But that's the same story everywhere.

To tell the truth, Klara would gladly stay in the villa a while longer. Right up to the wedding. If only Mrs. Hjort would bring up the subject. But Mrs. Hjort doesn't bring up the subject.


It's Saturday evening again. Fear and hope have alternated, rain and sun. The weather is turning warm. The new fragrance of a summer night unfolds fully over the earth. The maple is in blossom, the birdcherry and the cherry tree too. The balsam poplar around the bend perfumes the air.

A short rain has fallen. A breeze goes through the new foliage, a light rustle. Water droplets and maple tree flowers shower down briefly over Klara and Schjelderup, coming out of the open air dance together.

Klara is uneasy and dismayed. For one reason or another

everything is going wrong. Schjelderup hasn't been at all what she imagined. He's danced quite a lot with others and has been constantly joking, so she hasn't been able to really talk with him a single moment. Not until it was over did he suddenly appear to put his arm under hers, to kiss her and to whisper, "So how've you been since the last time I saw you, Klara?"

But Klara has suffered the pangs of jealousy all evening. It's so pleasant out here among all the villas this evening, so pretty. She dimly feels the injustice of having to leave the room facing the garden — the rosy lampshade was there and everything — and having to move into a back street photographer's. It's gray and unpleasant behind the screen in the studio. A rickety iron bed on uneven legs, a chipped wash basin and pitcher on a stand — that's all there is. She's not able now, at the drop of a hat, to be cheerful and affectionate toward Schjelderup. A little bitterly she supposes aloud that his love for her isn't genuine.

"Yes it is, of course it is," asserts Schjelderup. "You know it is, Klara. How can you think different, such a nice time we had together."

He explains to her that she shouldn't act silly now, she should be sweet like last time. As if he's supposed to figure out what's really wrong. Here he's gone around the whole week looking forward to seeing her, yes, and being alone with her — and now she's acting like this! But naturally, if she'd rather be rid of him, then —

Schjelderup's voice, the nearness of him, the hand that has slowly worked its way up over her arm and is now suddenly withdrawn, his last statement, hanging incomplete and threatening in the air, all of it together makes Klara's fragile little pride melt away. Deep down she doesn't want anything but to let it melt. She stops short. Damp blue eyes brimming over, she looks into Schjelderup's and announces that she's been fired.

"Oh hell," says Schjelderup.

"Yes, but I've already gone and got another place, you see," Klara calms him, not wanting to add to his burdens. "Temporarily," she says, "temporarily. And something else will probably turn up. If only you love me, Schjelderup. If only I can be sure of it."

Schjelderup passes right over this question. But he does ask what it's like where Klara's going next. Does she have her own room, for instance?

"In a way I do," answers Klara. But Schjelderup doesn't seem satisfied with that answer. He presses her further and it becomes apparent that the studio is inside the photographer's apartment. You have to walk through it.

A few vague thoughts stir in Klara's mind: now Schjelderup will figure something out, will find a solution. Perhaps now he'll say that. . . .

"It'll be difficult then — I mean to come and see you during the evening," says Schjelderup. He stands with his hands in his trouser pockets, staring into the distance and considering things.

Now he'll say it, the words pound in Klara's head; now he'll say that it's just as well we immediately. . . .

But a man often says something other than what a woman imagines he will. As Schjelderup does now. He stands rocking slightly on bent knees and explains, "Well, damned if I know for sure how things are going with me, either. They're starting a big building project someplace over on the west coast, I've heard. They're going to need a lot of people over there, they say. A couple of friends of mine and I were almost thinking of going over there. Not much is happening around these parts. Anyway, I thought I could go home with you tonight. So we could talk more about it."

"I don't dare, Schjelderup. I don't dare," whines Klara, crushed by his talk of moving on. In complete despair she clings to his neck. "You don't need to go way over there, do you? You surely don't need to go there. I wouldn't be able to see you for long stretches of time then. . . ."

She bores her face into Schjelderup's vest and howls, "Oh God, oh God, life is so hard."

Some distance away a group of young people, boys and girls, is coming down the road; they're laughing and yelling.

Schjelderup lifts his head and listens. Suddenly he pushes Klara's head and arms decisively away from his body; judging from everything, he's in a terrible hurry.

"Come on, Klara, thanks for the nice evening," he says quickly. "I hear someone over there I've absolutely got to talk to. I hope everything goes great with you...."

He moves off, swiftly and elastically, running with the skill of a fine athlete, becoming an unclear shadow, disappearing....

"Schjelderup," Klara calls, taking a few clumsy steps in her painful shoes after him down the road. Then she remains standing, arms hanging at her sides.

# *Lola*

S TARK  NAKED  she haunts my memory, affectedly putting
one foot forward and twisting her body, snapping her fingers
like castanets and making her nostrils quiver. She's snatched a
rose from the bowl on the table, just like that, and stuck it in
her hair, behind her ear. I see it clear enough. Her audacity is
boundless. She gropes for my hand, wants to kiss it and thus
disarm me completely.

I am about to banish her. Back to the depths of oblivion
from which she emerged. Who was Lola? A little ninny, who
bluffed, lied and made scenes – cunning, bold, inconsiderate –
sweet too, of course – ugly and picturesque. All in all, a pain
in the neck, who left chaos and confusion in her wake.

Then she slaps herself on the thigh so it crackles. "*Espagnole*," she cries, with triumph in her voice.

And, as if on film in a developing solution, appear, more
or less distinctly, the people to whom her cry is directed. A
little group of Scandinavians who pay through the nose to
sketch Lola in the nude. With drawing boards supported on
their knees, they sit on stools, take sights and measures, squint,
run charcoal and punk in inspired arcs over the paper. At the
cry they look up, they exchange glances and smile. Şmiles that
express mixed emotions. They may dwell on their solid and
reliable qualities, but they also must remember their inertia
and repression, how heavy their spirits can be.

One of them gets up, a tall, fair figure with an almost white
shock of hair. He goes over and corrects Lola's position, which
became disarranged when she slapped herself on the thigh.

She's thoughtless that way, Lola; she's impulsive and Spanish. In jest she snaps for his hand and misses it, then gets hold of it from another angle and places her cheek against it. He reddens so that his countless freckles drown and disappear a moment, while everyone laughs. Jens Olsen from Gamvik in Finnmark, Norway. "Blond, blond, he's blond," says Lola. She sticks a finger in his hair to see if it's for real and pouts like a child when he goes.

There's the Swedish woman painter in the striped, hand-woven dress, Vadstena collar and brooch of hammered copper. The Danish woman with the Madonna-like hair and elegant air. The Norwegian woman, who hasn't yet learned how to use powder, but manages as best she can, with far too much on the tip of her nose. Pär. Quite distinctly I see Pär, a Småländer* who, after two years residence in Paris, still goes around in a cocoon of homespun, in heavy farm shoes and an oafish haircut, not in the least corrupted by the big city, inside or out. I see Jens distinctly too, his eyes blue and absent-minded, fantastically unassuming, a dreamer from Gamvik. There he is, making his big speech to Lola in his northern Norwegian dialect – he, the man of few words. But by then they were finished with her; by then the cup had run over.

Distinctly I see the picture he painted, built up, scraped and slapped together, seemingly produced through a succession of catastrophes, huge and unforgettable.

Most distinctly of all I see Lola herself. She holds up her index finger, opens her eyes wide and says self-importantly, "*Ma mère, vous savez...!*" And has with that evoked a figure, invisible certainly, but to be reckoned with.

Lola carries on in every respect like a star. She's constantly making herself the center of attention; she can't jump up or down from the model's table once without doing something or other. It's a bow to one and all, then it's kisses blown in every direction. Then she dances around the atelier, hunting for her

---

*A very provincial Swede. – Trans.

music portfolio – Lola has a music portfolio – finds it, pulls out a scribbled piece of paper, asks for a few moments' attention. Then, naked as God created her, she reads aloud a poem by Verlaine or Maurice Magre, by one important poet or another, living or dead; she ends with the modest, "This is by me. Tell me frankly what you think. Inspiration came over me this morning. That's the reason I was so late."

What do they think? They are speechless. Even Pär smells trouble and looks alarmed. *"Très joli,"* says the Danish woman painter finally, when the silence threatens to become oppressive.

This takes place in a sidestreet in Montparnasse, in Pär's atelier, large and run down and so overgrown with ivy that its long tentacles have worked their way in here and there. When there's a wind they move around.

It takes place in bygone days. Before the war.

I see morning scenes, many morning scenes. Lola arrives too late, always too late, far too late. It's not even certain that she'll come at all. The others wander around, turn over Pär's studies, arranged along the walls on the floor, and set them back in place; they grow listless, drained, empty.

At last she stands in the doorway, brimming with explanations. These never fail her – on the contrary. The amazing thing is that she has overcome all obstacles and arrived.

*"O, là, là,"* cries Lola, while she dashes around, kissing the women's hands and cordially slapping the men on the shoulder. "What don't I do for you, my friends, what don't I put up with?" Once again Lola had to pass through Neuilly – or Etoiles, Passy, Auteuil – fine faraway suburbs – in order to reach the more modest Montparnasse. Or she's worked the whole morning, writing, composing; the inspiration came over her, for her calling in life isn't to be a model, far from it. She is exhausted, destroyed, finished. But she had promised to show up and isn't one of those to break a promise.

All the while she's stripping off her clothes. They fly in all directions around her, a garment here, a garment there. *"Là, là, là, là, là, là, là."* She hops up onto the model's table, twists her body into an ever-new position, into something astonishing they've never seen before. If they ask where she's gotten it from, she answers, "From my dances." She clicks her tongue as if to a team of horses and cries delightedly, "*C'est chic, hein?*" They're already sitting there, bent over their drawing boards, nervous, productive. Lola is, after all, no ordinary model with slack, conventional positions, an eternal at-ease stance and hands up behind her neck. She's quick and fiery, with unexpected lines, like a fish in the water when she gets her clothes off. She has large eyes like prunes, surrounded by thick layers of blue and black; a big, red-lacquered mouth, a broad flat nose, a face whose width is gloriously distorted and so white with powder that it catches reflections as a white-washed wall does, becoming clear light green or violet, or brick red in the shadows, all according to her surroundings. Her mane is thick and woolly, changing from copper to soot; her limbs heavy, the legs two strong bundles of muscles. They could hold up a big, powerful woman; they hold up a little, sinewy, sand-gray torso. Lola seems to have escaped from one or another of the era's typical paintings, seems to have climbed down from the wall of the "Independents" or the "Fauves" room at the Autumn Salon. She claims to have posed for Van Dongen and Matisse — in secret, naturally, as her life consists of secrets. It's not the most improbable thing Lola has ever said. Her success as a model she explains in these words, "*On me trouve drôle, voilà.*" And her nostrils quiver, moving like a forest animal's.

Lola's father, said to be deceased, has at times been a doctor, at times an engineer. Lola's mother, on the other hand, is at all times from old Spanish nobility and made, in point of fact, a misalliance. With a black man, one might think, seeing Lola's flat nose and woolly hair. But if there's anything she consistently sticks to, it's her Spanish heritage. "*Espagnole!*" she cries and slaps her thigh. It's as if she'cried, "Top that if you can!"

She has an amazing power over the little group of people from the North. Without protest they allow themselves to be crammed full of stories, made fools of and pumped for money in advance. Don't they stand there and dig into their thin wallets and pool their resources again? Even though it isn't Saturday.

Even Pär is under Lola's spell. Pär, the farmer who isn't impressed by anything. "Full of tricks," he mumbles after her. "Full of the devil." It's not meant as censure.

They had been like all penniless youth in foreign capitals, outside everything. They were diligent, tramped through museums and sat in sidewalk cafés, looking as experienced as they could. They acquired dangerous habits to the extent it was possible — an apertif here and there, a little exaggerated smoking, a leg nonchalantly crossed over the other, elbows on the table. They were outsiders all the same. Their work became pure drudgery, just as it had been at home, with the boring monotony of the academy and everyday unromantic hardships. No easy escape, no intoxication. And then came Lola.

Gorgeously colorful, gorgeously exaggerated with a past set in Marseilles and Rio, where Lola had passed through on her way from Martinique, across the sea. Not in order to become a model or to perform — no, no. Forced by necessity, behind her relatives' backs and with catastrophes hanging over her head, she plies this trade and calls it music lessons. The world is wicked and the path of genius strewn with thorns. To find publishers for her poems and compositions, to create a career for herself as an artist and to ensure her mother a genteel old age — those were the reasons she started out.

Something no one believes, not even Pär. But behind it all even he suspects mysteries of another kind. Which kind isn't easy to say. Secrets, the unknown circumstances of life.


Jens' painting of her thrusts itself into the foreground, obtrusively distinct.

"Mine is the big format," Jens said. "The colossal format. Paintbrushes can never be long enough or wide enough. Normal size is no size at all."

That's a belief he has. Like all beliefs it demands sacrifice. Only periodically do Jens' watch and chain decorate his person. Likewise his overcoat, even when November may have set in with raw and incessant rain. Jens doesn't eat many meals out, but buys cooked beans and other cheap food to bring home, goes to bed early to save light and is the inventor of a heating system that is essentially powered by ashes. None of this seems to be hard for him except being without a watch. When it's gone Jens usually arrives too early for everything. Never too late. Every time he gets money from home, it's in order that he use it to come home. In Gamvik they think that there's been just about enough of Parisian life. Jens uses the money to stay on.

Number two in his articles of belief sounds like this: "If I were rich I'd give money for *supplies* to student painters. So they wouldn't be required to scrimp on *them* anyway." He can say that, blue in the face with cold, at the same time he squeezes out whole tubes of cadmium and madder on the palatte and slaps on the expensive colors as if he were mortaring bricks.

Third belief: "What I'm going to paint someday is Northern Norway. Then they'll see *breadth*. No one has ever painted it the way it should be painted. Well, I only want to try. It's not certain I can manage it either."

There he is, dragging along a rectangular canvas, so large it covers his whole body, except his head and feet, when he carries it in front of him. He looks like a mast with the square sail up, navigating laboriously to find a better spot. He's got to have space, enough room to turn around. He's thoroughly in the way, making tempers fly wherever he goes.

"You're mad," they say. "Stop going on this way."

"You have this week, not a single day longer. Just so you know..."

"He won't have even covered the canvas..."

"And then, Lola, well...Lola!"

"He'll have to take the responsibility himself."

The others go around with small, suitable canvases, sight-ing, measuring, squinting, making frames with their fingers, as they look through them at Lola. A quick study is all they attempt. For many reasons. Jens has a screw loose.

"Yes, yes, yes," says Jens. "Yes, I hear you."

This is what it's come to — Lola is going to be painted. It was bound to come to this. Not that Lola has anything against it. She's made them aware of the risks she runs in being away from home four hours a day instead of two. On the other hand, it's during the third or fourth hour that something is achieved in art; she knows that well herself. And what won't she do for her friends?

She lies on Pär's divan. On a blanket with large flowers, faded, dirty and worn, but with the colors all the finer for it. She makes her nostrils quiver, clicks her tongue and, not least, gives Jens her praise. "*He* is an artist. *He* sees the big picture. *He* is daring. *He* isn't afraid."

She arches herself backwards with her arms under her head in the pre-determined way. "*C'est chic, hein?* Go ahead, my friends."

They go ahead. And in doing so make themselves even more dependent on her than before. The innocent souls from the North. Not quite so innocent as Lola believes; in their own eyes anything but innocent. Yet they might as well be.


I see Jens making great brush strokes on his canvas, so that it's dangerous to go near him. In a couple of days he has covered an unbelievable area. Color he flings on in clumps, fine colors, expensive colors, no cheap, decorative stuff. He keeps away from Veronese green because it darkens with age and he cleans his palette thoroughly after every use — he doesn't just throw it heedlessly up on a nail. As long as it's up to Jens, his work will last centuries.

Finally he stands with his legs far apart, drying the cleaned brushes on a rag and examining his work. He has an expression around his mouth that's new to him.

At every break Lola is up, inspecting herself. She walks

around politely to one and all and says encouraging things. But it's at Jens' side that she remains standing. It's there she cries from a full heart, "I can really inspire people."

She doesn't stand there alone. Everyone stands there.

Jens' Lola is an overwhelming Lola, a Lola you can only bow down to. In powder-blue and pink, in ochre and gray, in curves and angles, against a background as fantastic as a dream jungle. The prune eyes almost touch the ears, as does the lacquered mouth. The background is just as generously painted, with finger-thick black outlines wherever you look. It's Jens' expression of Jens' impression of Lola, beautiful in her own vehement way and completely for her own sake.

Lola throws out her arms in both directions. "Everyone here will be a great artist, a *great* artist. But that one there, the blond, he'll be the master." She kisses Jens' fingers and promises him fame, fortune, love in the future.

"I'd be content if you just came on time in the morning, you wretch," mumbles Jens in his northern dialect.


Lola doesn't come on time. Jens, on the other hand, has begun to arrive almost an hour too early. He doesn't have his watch and besides that he's doing battle with his motif and longs to be working. He's let in; as a comrade and notorious genius he can demand that. It's no longer a question of Jens' justifying his undertaking. It's a question of standing by him. He drags his painting around, sets it up, first here, then there, in different lights. Every now and then he collides with Pär, who must shave and get the stove going and who would like to wander around with his own sketch. Finally both of them drift from wall to wall, without saying much, and things grow undeniably tedious. In distraction Jens moves Pär's canvases, looks at them briefly and places them so carelessly against the wall that Pär has to come over and see that they're all right, that no harm has come to them. The others arrive one by one and walk around in the same fashion. The one week has become three, going on four.

One morning a scene takes place. Not between Pär and Jens, but between Pär and Lola. In his scanty French Pär asks suddenly if it wouldn't be possible to move the music lessons to Montparnasse to save time. Lola flies straight at Pär and scratches him on the hand, which he's put up in front of his face at the last minute.

Jens places himself between them and Lola throws, for lack of anything else, a shoe after Pär, calls him a swine and a camel and worse, assuring him in a rush of words that a lady like her mother never sets foot in a dirty neighborhood like this, is not *permitted* to set foot here.

"Now, now, now," everyone says. "Come, Pär," they say. But Pär stands there sucking his scratches; he looks over at Lola and mutters, "Damned kid." It's not only in rebuke.

Lola breaks into loud, angry crying. But after a moment she's herself again and she sweetly begs Pär's pardon. It makes her head spin just to think about what could happen. Her mother could disown her, turn white-haired overnight, kill herself, come here and make scenes, bring suit against them all for seducing a minor, all this from the mere sight of streets like these. "I'm not twenty-one," says Lola and looks around darkly. "She would understand *everything*. *Voilà*."

Silence.

That day Lola has to leave before her time is up. She jumps down suddenly from the model's table, runs around looking for her clothes, has to hurry. She can't say why, but it would be an act of unparalleled irresponsibility to stay longer this particular day. Moreover, she has to have another advance, even though she got one the other day. A matter of precaution, purely a matter of precaution.

Jens sits down on Pär's woodbox, pale and exhausted under his freckles. He's just scraped away a whole arm and a big piece of the background. With a hard, bitter expression he looks fixedly at Lola.

She comes over and says something to him in a low voice. But then she leaves.

"Pär!" sounds from all sides.

"Well?" says Pär guiltily.

"You know how it is with Lola and her music lessons. And with her mother and everything...."

"Oh...."

But everyone agrees that if Pär were going to make scenes he should have done it before. They shouldn't be happening now; he should restrain himself.

"For how long then?" Pär challenges them.

They look around. At their overworked sketches. At each other. They've exchanged places, used up all the possibilities, are on the verge of ruin. But it's not possible to let Jens down. His painting has virtually been accepted by the salon. They imagine it in a place of honor, see people gathering in front of it....

"One week more," someone says.

"One," cries Jens. "I might as well go throw myself in the ocean. I might as well go straight to the ocean."

"Two, then," comes resignedly from another corner.

Neither Pär nor Jens answers. After a while Pär says, "I don't give a damn."

This is understood to mean that he accepts it.


But one day Lola turns up far too late, enveloped in a long black veil like a widow. "What's going on now?"

"Count So and So is dead," explains Lola quietly and pronounces a long, complex Spanish name with "y" between all the different parts. "He was a close relative on my mother's side. I'm in mourning."

She unfolds the day's paper and points out a few lines that do indeed announce that Count So and So is dead.

General consternation of the sort that arises when Lola reads Verlaine aloud, saying "This is by me."

"*Très triste*," the Danish woman painter finally says, when the silence threatens to become oppressive.

"He was the only one in the family who stood by my mother when she married my father," explains Lola. She dries,

as if surreptitiously, a treacherous tear, takes off her clothes
without any antics or funny business and assumes her position.
Everyone works nervously. No one says anything.

During the break Lola bursts into tears over by the door,
where she's placed her clothes for the occasion, nicely folded
in a pile; she finds a pocket handkerchief and sniffles into it.

In wonder and perplexity the others look on. It can't be
serious, can it?

But Lola is crying for her mother's sake, first and foremost
for her mother's sake. Who doesn't have clothes to wear to the
funeral, or money to send a wreath. Lola has gone into debt to
get mourning veils for both of them, has paid the house rent
and other large bills, is without a sou. How to get a lady of the
old school, so innocent in her pride, so blind in her trust of
Lola to comprehend this? When Lola is gone for four hours,
she's ostensibly had four music students and earned four times
as much as she has in reality. At least four times. Ahh, life is
tragic. You keep your head up, you act carefree, but there are
moments. . . .

She finishes with hard-won calm, "I shouldn't bother you
with this, my friends. Forgive me my weakness. But – *if* I don't
come tomorrow, forgive me that, too. It's not the will that is
lacking but strength giving way."

Everyone looks involuntarily at Jens. He's put down his
palette and stands there with his arms crossed, his eyes blue
and hard. He says, "There's only one solution for me, and
that's to go jump in the ocean."

He looks at Lola as he did the other day – contemptuous
and angry.

Something like an impending catastrophe is brewing in
the air. Even if Jens doesn't seriously go out and tramp those
many miles to the ocean, he may do some other desperate thing
– slash his canvas, for instance. This city has a large river
flowing through it; what if he's thinking about that? This is no
longer a joke.

Jens has been looking worn out lately too, thin and bony;
it's even more pronounced right now. The muscles in his face

have become strangely conspicuous, tightening like knots on each side of his mouth.

Lola goes over and talks to him in a low voice, as she's done before. And once again, however it happens, the upshot is that they pool their money; they turn their wallets inside out once again. But they won't be able to do it much longer. Their finances won't allow it.

Lola overflows with thanks. She will never forget this, never let them down; she'll pose for them for free, pose longer than she's obliged to. She becomes suddenly and completely herself again, snaps her fingers and does a dance step, but catches herself. It was only that she was so relieved.... She holds up her index finger, "*Ma mère, vous savez....*"

Don't misunderstand — her mother is an angel. A true angel. But she's from the Spanish nobility; she's proud. Just thinking of her daughter alone in the streets is a torment. Every morning she follows Lola, stands watching her daughter disappear into elegant houses, sits by the hour in parks and waits for her to come out again — as much as four hours and more, my friends — all in the innocent belief that these are music lessons. After a great deal of struggle she has acquiesced to Lola giving music lessons, to her teaching. Ah — to deceive her mother — to keep her mother in the dark! But better that than to see her go to bed hungry....

Here Lola breaks off. Jens is staring at her, insistent and blue-eyed and bitter. She stops talking and the work goes on for a while.


Then came the memorable morning when Lola arrived so inordinately late. Close to two hours late. When Jens, the taciturn Jens, told her off in northern Norwegian. An ill-fated morning.

With his long legs stretched out across the floor, his hands thrust to the bottom of his trouser pockets and his shoulders hunched, Jens sits on Pär's woodbox, knotting the muscles around his mouth, silent. Everyone is silent. When a man has staked everything on one card and it looks like it's going to lose, what's there to say? Whenever she wants Lola can stay away for good. She has nothing owing to her, just the opposite. As far as where she lives, she never reveals her address to anyone. "We live a completely retired life. Because of our position."

Suddenly she stands in the doorway, blushing under her powder, out of breath, excited. Before anyone can utter a reproachful word, she snaps her fingers. "*Ça y est* — I've got a part!"

Silence.

"You don't share my happiness?" cries Lola. "Me — who takes part in everything that concerns you!"

With hands on her hips she walks across the room. "Don't think this is a simple walk-on part. Three entrances, with verses and dancing, my own credit line on the poster, my own dressing rooms, costumes from — well, you wouldn't know the firm. I've just come from the audition. I'm exhausted, but you see I won't let you down. All the time I can spare you can continue to see me. The director is crazy about me, but I'm keeping him at a distance...."

Pause.

"And your mother?" someone asks. "What does she say?"

"My mother!" Lola thinks about it a second, no longer. "For her it's a blow. But she's resigned herself."

"You really were a musician. And a poet?"

"Poetry, music, song, dance, I have them all in my blood. I'm an artist, an artist! But aren't you happy for me, my friends?"

"No, damned if we are. We'd be glad if you sat in hell's kitchen, you devil, you and your noble mother. Because people like you ruin everything in life. I don't know what sort of role you've gotten and it doesn't matter, it's probably nothing very important. But I do know you've taken our money and our time and our good faith in the most shameful way. You should be ashamed of yourself! Music lessons. Your mother said music lessons too, every time she came to see me, wanting to borrow ten francs or five francs — or even one franc. You think that because of this picture you can keep taking and taking advantage of us, but this is the end now. Damned if it's not the end! Fools we may be, but not such fools that we don't understand what a pack of villains you are, you and your mother and your lover, sitting over there at the café on the corner waiting for you and our money. That's enough now. You can go now. And *stay* away. We don't respect you any longer, you poor wretch.

"And you," Jens turns to the others. "Yes, now you know. I've been a prize sap. For the sake of this painting. This wretched painting. First it was saving the old family jewels, then this, then that. I don't remember now what it wasn't. I've been a sap, like I said. For the sake of the painting. It wasn't for any other reason, don't you dare believe it...."

This, or something like it, is what Jens says, all in a rush without stopping and in his northern Norwegian dialect. He goes over and takes the canvas down from the easel, stands fumbling with it and hides his face as best he can. He's ashamed. It's wet as a boy's.

Lola isn't stupid. Not bad either. Just hopeless. She hasn't grasped a word but has understood, all the same, and perhaps acknowledged it. She walks over, takes Jens' hand and wants to kiss it. He shoves her away. He maneuvers himself out the door with his creation.

It's terrible.


But a little later, when Lola quietly disappeared, it was terrible too.

She went her way and was no longer anything but a brazen and cunning little swindler, a small-timer, who hadn't been brazen and cunning *enough*.

Her mystique was the mystique of millions of little bubble-heads. The whole earth is full of them and they're not that remarkable, even if they are from Martinique. She was a pain in the neck and would never be anything else, and you could thank your lucky stars to be rid of her.

But all the same...

They missed Lola.

# *Papen*

PAPEN WAS A PARROT who over the years traveled more widely than most.

I first remember him against a background of the red parlor walls of 49 Huitfeldtsgate and of mother's scarlet runners, lobelia and nasturtium on the balcony.

It was June and warm. The balcony doors stood open. The sun streamed in. Papen chattered animatedly, excited by our voices. He ruffled his feathers, flapped his wings and looked like he was supposed to – gorgeous and tropical.

We children flew in and out, feeling self-important about him and about the other things that had appeared in our house. Father was home again from the sea. That was synonymous with the new and exciting things all around the room. We also had a completely new little brother, and we had moved. There was no end to it.

Impressed friends followed in our wake, among the group a black girl. She was what was new and interesting in another family, had been brought from Africa, with the best intentions, to be raised in Christian self-abnegation in Norway. In time, things turned out differently for her than her benefactors had imagined.

Somewhere in the warm, colorful picture I see, like a thin gray streak, Grandfather from Trondheim, skinnier than anyone else, who'd also come to look and marvel. We run through the room. Grandfather from Trondheim gets up from his after-dinner nap, rubs his eyes, bewildered, and asks, "Do you have Negroes, too?"

*

I remember Papen downhearted, eyes closed longsuffer-
ingly, puffed up and looking like a green ball of feathers with
a beak.
He sits in his cage in front of a window. It's very far north.
Maybe there's a snowstorm outside, maybe the window panes
are frosted.
Or there's sunshine night and day. The eternal snow cap
on the mountain peak at the farthest end of the fjord is glowing;
the eddies in the channel outside are sparkling with gold.
Papen is bored. Only at mealtimes does he get a little
amusement, or when someone casually goes through the room
and stops by his cage. Father does it most often and keeps it
up longest, but he doesn't have much time. For us children
Papen has little by little become more a part of the furniture
than a living being. We're busy with everything else. And
Mother has a thousand things to think about.
I remember him the last time in front of another window,
typical of houses built in the 1890s in Oslo. A big bay window
overlooking a courtyard.
Papen is old. Mostly he sits and sleeps, with his head under his wing.


He is the animal I've known longest of all. And at the same
time the one I've known least. I don't think that anyone knew
Papen. He eventually became strange and eccentric. No one
can know an eccentric.
Father brought him home from South America when I
was eight or nine. He stayed with us for another forty years.
He stayed in the family, that is. He ended his life at my aunts',
at 12 Elisenbergveien, where he one day, most unexpectedly,
died in a corner of the sofa. Certainly not of boredom. During
his last year he was, on the contrary, the object of three nice
old ladies' untiring thoughtfulness. But good fortune sometimes comes to us too late.
Before Papen arrived, Father wrote to us that he had with
him two monkeys and a parrot. The monkeys, poor things,

died on the way, to Mother's indescribable relief. We children saw it differently. The bigger the menagerie we had in the house, the better.

Papen came to Norway on the corvette *Ellida*. Consequently he said *Ellida* at every opportunity. He also said hello in varying tones of voice, as well as a couple of Portuguese sentences from his homeland. Father laughed when Papen came out with them, but would never say what they meant.

Father had bought him on the streets of Bahia. There he sat, chained to his perch. Throughout his life he retained around his leg a ring you couldn't get off. On board ship he had been allowed to go freely everywhere, and eventually he became quite tame and fond of people.

Like all naval officers at that time Father had whiskers. They went with the uniform.

I remember Papen sitting on his shoulder, tugging lightly and playfully on his whiskers and chattering in parrot language with a low, soft voice. That language has many pleasant little words and sounds.

He also sat willingly on our hands, bit us a little on the fingers, but not so it hurt, cocked his head and prattled quietly when he wanted to be scratched on the neck. He was young, we could see that by his beak; it wasn't black yet. But whether, in fact, he was gentleman, or a lady, is unclear to this day.

From Horten to Oslo Papen traveled in a hatbox with holes in the lid. In Drammen Father went into the station to eat. When he came back, he heard high, animated hellos from the train compartment. There sat Papen on the rim of the hat box, triumphant at getting out of his prison, greeting his fellow travelers elatedly and incessantly.

At first we let him go freely. A high stand with crosswise perches that the carpenter onboard had made for him was

Papen's baggage when he arrived. The idea was for him to stay there and climb up and down.

They say that parrots are climbing birds and don't fly very much. Ours flew. Not high, not around very widely, but often and gladly. One time he even flew so far we thought we'd never see him again.

But to begin with he stayed within the four walls of the house and was wild enough there.

He flew, for example, up on the piano and left a mess. Then he fluttered away to a table and left another. And parrot messes are no joke. Mother came running, the househelp came running. Ugh, they said. Ick, they said. How in the world did they stand this onboard? they said.

Talking to Papen about these matters was no use. Mother said, I'll have to talk to Fabricius.

But Fabricius had a weak spot for Papen. Nothing was done that time.

He liked to walk on the floor. And if he had stayed there he probably never would have been put in a cage. Not so long as it was summer anyway and the rugs were up. It's no great accident if something happens on a painted floor, and even the househelp thought it was pleasant to have him going in and out. You heard a strange little noise of claws on wood in the room and Papen came into view, green and yellow, red and blue, with his head cocked, and horribly pigeon-toed. He looked up at us with one eye and chattered.

But then he recalled he was a climbing bird and that there are other possibilities besides stands with perches. Curtains, among other things.

To swing back and forth as if on jungle lianas, and to let himself glide down in a long slash was quite effortless. It was also entertaining to sit on the back of a chair, tear off pieces of wallpaper with his beak and throw them around.

Much was forgiven Papen, because he was so affectionate

and nice and soon learned to say poor Papen, softly and compas-
sionately at the appropriate times. But one day Mother cried.
Fabricius had to go downtown and return in a taxi with the
biggest cage he could find. He preferred that to chaining Papen
to the perch, and he was probably right.


To begin with, Papen took the whole thing as if it were a
joke of an idea, a kind of guessing game thought up for his
amusement. Steadily he worked on the lock and, time after
time, sat in the open door, saying hello, poor Papen and *Ellida*,
then flying over to the nearest table and making a mess.

A device with steel thread was fixed up, but Papen taught
himself to pick that open too. In a book on bird care I've since
read, it says that those sorts of parrots are often very ingenious.
Papen was, no doubt about it.

Locking him up completely never worked. Whatever we
tried, he would get out sooner or later. But gradually he resigned himself to staying in the cage, sitting in the door opening, or climbing on his roof. Disappointed in people, Papen
retreated from them. When, during the course of the years, he
sometimes lifted his wings and flew, it was as if in a delirium,
as if in a dream. He himself looked more surprised than anyone
when he landed after such a flight.

We, too, become different when we're put in cages. Not
to mention how we'd change if we lived for forty years among
only parrots, never seeing a human being. Not easy to be
around, of that I'm certain.

Everything taken into consideration, Papen was really a
noble and lenient bird. It was good of him not to become more
crotchety than he did.

For we treated him, in good faith, very foolishly and very
badly.


His nature was to see everything in the best light. He

didn't even understand at first that teasing could be more than pure fun.

Uncle Bastian teased Papen. Or, better said, pushed the comic to a point not far from teasing in my eyes.

I also saw the humor of Papen. But behind it I saw, then as now, the tragic, saw the painful and inexplicable, the way children perceive things like that.

I liked Uncle Bastian otherwise. He had a sense of humor; there was always fun and high spirits when he came. But he shouldn't have made a fool of Papen. I became angry with him, I asked God to make him want to be better, even to make him stop coming. I went to bed even more unwillingly than usual when he was around. He was the kind you had to keep your eye on.

I'm sure he lived in happy ignorance of all that, probably never even noticing how sulky I was.

I didn't dare say anything. We were well brought up in those days. All too well brought up.


Papen was never very adept at human speech, but that was our fault. We neglected his education.

He was, as I've said, a gifted bird and he taught himself, on his own, quite a lot — our names, among other things. His hello came out often in inappropriate places, but also always in the right ones, when anyone entered the room or there was a knocking at the door. When we laughed, Papen laughed, shrilly and like a crazy person. When the piano was being played, in our apartment or elsewhere in the building, he broke into song, piercingly off-key, so excited and eager that he hopped back and forth on his perch.

All that happened at our home in Huitfeldtsgate. He had his best days there, hadn't yet experienced any long, sunless, arctic winters and hadn't had his courage dashed.

From the balcony Papen called whoa to the horses, so that they halted. To the great delight of the children in the street,

to the lesser joy of the drivers. "That damned bird up there."
That was before the automobile's time, and even though the
neighborhood was quiet and didn't swarm with either animals
or people, there were quite a few opportunities to call whoa.
The milkman, coalman, woodseller and breadman used horses,
and we sometimes saw a cab.

The neighbors were patient people. When the windows
were open or the cage out on the balcony, Papen must have
been about as trying for the neighborhood as a loudspeaker today. But I never remember anyone complaining.


It was also in Huitfeldtsgate that Papen set in motion his
fantastic attempt at escape.

The cage was out on the balcony one day. And the cage
was empty. Once again Papen had managed to pick open one
of our ingenious steel thread knots. One we'd believed he
would never get undone.

A great stir.

What isn't a living being capable of, when freedom is at
stake? Papen, who generally flew rather low to the ground and
in short little stretches like a fluttering hen, was now so completely out of sight that it was impossible to find him either
upstairs or downstairs. Not in any of the other balconies, not
in the trees across the street in the vacant lot.

It was terrible. We children cried. Imagine if Papen didn't
come home by nightfall! Imagine if he never came home and
maybe got caught by a cat! A reward of five kroner – a sizeable
sum in those days – was promised to whoever brought Papen
back or found out where he was.

All the children on the block sprang into action. We searched
everywhere, in the courtyard, in the backyards and in the
vacant lots that were the great delight of our childhood. We
rang front doorbells. The one who finally, when it was almost
evening, actually found Papen, was a stranger, a young boy
who was walking by the Heftyes garden and heard a hello
called from a tree.

Papen had succeeded in flying all the way there. He had covered the lower part of Huitfeldtsgate and crossed Munke-damsveien. It was incomprehensible.

As he sat there in the foliage, he believed perhaps that it was beginning to look like the jungle again, and he called to the other parrots. His mother tongue got mixed up with what he'd learned in the foreign one. That's easy for any of us to do when we've been away long.

The boy understood that something wasn't right. The voice was peculiar, as well as the place it came from. It was a matter here of catching a fugitive.

So he did. The children who'd been running around searching showed him where Papen belonged. He came home in a great procession.

But the boy was badly bit in the hand, had to be bandaged after the struggle and to be paid in excess of his reward. Papen hadn't given himself up without a fight. Something anyone can agree with.

After that we were careful about leaving Papen on the balcony or in rooms with open windows.

I can still hear Mother's "I'm opening a window in here, move Papen."

Until the time when, with the years, he became so unenterprising that he could no longer be suspected of anything.


It's not easy to say when his transformation to eccentric began in earnest. It could have been after his attempt at escape.

He got into the habit of moving away on his perch when we wanted to scratch his neck, of chattering after us when we went by, as if he couldn't stand the sight, of clamping himself onto the bars of the cage, flapping his wings and making a continual cry. Either he was desperately calling to other parrots or he simply wanted to protest wildly.

In any case, he eventually became a completely different bird, unpredictable, annoyingly loud and unreliable. Eccentric is too mild a word. Hysteric is how we label people like that.

He was, as I've said, a well-traveled parrot.

It wasn't enough that he came from South America to Norway. From Oslo he went far, far north, and even traveled on his own around the coast to Trondheim.

The cage was too big to have in the train compartment. The dark baggage car we found too gloomy, especially since it was early in the year and cold. Papen was put on board the boat that was taking our furniture and an agreement made with the captain and restaurant manager.

He traveled in the first class salon and, as far as that goes, comfortably. We believed the holy relic to be in good keeping. But when we met Papen again he was, quite simply, angry; you couldn't get near him, he scolded and fumed. The cage looked disgusting. All sorts of food had been pushed inside for him, but no one had dared to clean it for many days.

It couldn't have been just life at sea. He knew the sea from before and had shown himself to be an able-bodied sailor. It wasn't the strange surroundings either. Papen was at that time still a sociable bird, who gladly made friends with anyone who came forward.

A traveling salesman had been badly bitten in the hand, however, and was wearing a bandage, something he'd certainly earned. A little dog was so afraid of Papen that its entire body shook just to be in the salon with him. It was other people's fault, not the dog's. Certain people only know one way to act around animals – taunting them with each other.

On the trip further north Papen came with us. That was before the days of the express ships. It took us a week; we went into every possible fjord and we anchored at night. Papen had time to become more or less his old self again and showed us, in all sorts of ways, his happiness at seeing us again.

It was sleeting one early morning as we docked at the town where we were going to live. With the cage, wrapped in a wool blanket, at the head, we filed through the empty quiet streets. Inside the blanket we heard Papen reflecting over it all in parrot language.

Father said, "Here comes the Circus Madigan."*


All who live outside their natural states become changed in time, whether they sit in cages or not. To his other peculiarities Papen added such strange eating habits that he would have been regarded as a great original if he had returned to the jungle. Not that he could have managed there, either. His habits had become human.

He developed a taste for coffee, drank it neatly from a teaspoon that he held in one claw. He loved jam and ate it in the same way. If he saw cutlets on the table, he cried and nagged until he got a bone that he also held up by a claw and picked clean with enormous appetite. Between bites he let his relish be known in parrot language.

His place was in front of a dining room window. He kept a watchful eye on everything that appeared on the table and loudly demanded his share. There was never any doubt about what he did or didn't want. Whatever wasn't satisfactory he threw away in contempt, shrieking once again until he got his way. Hempseeds — his own food — he almost never touched. Sugar lumps between the bars remained unnoticed, but everything we had, he wanted to taste. Parsley was the exception. We'd heard it was deadly poison to parrots.

In the beginning we were afraid to give him all that people food. But, as nothing happened, we almost forgot that he wasn't one of us. We thought it was fun.

In reality it was merely stupid and can have been part of what made Papen the way he was — irritable and bad-humored. People are what they eat, someone has said; parrots certainly are too. Fruit, rice, macaroni, potatoes and those sorts of things weren't harmful, but coffee was, very much so. And cutlet bones were just plain dangerous. Papen could have become a feather-eater that way, one of the worst things that can happen

---

*A well-known Scandinavian circus. — Trans.

to a parrot. That's when they pluck at themselves until they sit there naked and wretched. Our Papen escaped such a humiliating condition. It wasn't owing to his guardians; it came from his own healthy nature.

After a while meals became the only regular distraction Papen had. The grown-ups had more and more to think about, and less and less time. We children grew up and away from Papen.

We liked him in an unthinking way. No one went past the cage without making a gesture of scratching his neck for a minute. He knew that wasn't much to count on and preferred to sit where he was, barely cracking open an eye and then closing it again.

Sometimes he was in a sentimental mood. Then he came up to the bars and demonstrated that he, for his part, didn't hold a grudge. In the absence of parrots he longed for people and was amicable as long as possible.

But he could also, in pure desperation, cling to the bars with his beak, flap his wings and shriek furiously to draw our attention. If we talked to him a little and said, "Now, now, what a clever bird," he calmly went and sat down again, muttering in parrot language, "You see, that's how I have to exert myself to make you remember I exist."

Naturally he still remained an unusual and rare object. No one else owned anything like him. He was the town's only parrot – we knew that for a certainty.

"Do you want to come in and see Papen?" was an invitation that was always successful, and even won us friends. When we thronged about his cage and he heard new voices Papen must have believed many times that his loneliness was at an end. He puffed up his feathers, ran back and forth on the perch, joined loudly and animatedly in the conversation. He did what we expected of him and performed. He broke wildly into his crazy laughter when we laughed.

We heard him call after us when we left.

\*

At intervals of years he lifted up his wings and flew. To his own and others' surprise.

One time stands out clearly in my mind. My youngest brother was going to a dance. He had striven mightily with the part in his hair and, at the last minute, came through the dining room, holding out his white-gloved fingers and so afraid for his coiffure that he called to the rest of us, "Don't come near me, don't come near me."

It was Papen who came near. He sat in the door of his cage, lifted his wings in flight and landed in the middle of that fine, newly brushed hair, tousling it completely before he got his claws free and flew away again.

Papen shared our malicious pleasure with enthusiasm.


One time we were given touching proof of how lonely he was.

The food in the cage began to disappear. Everything was gone, even the hempseeds and the sugar lump. But Papen himself, who'd gotten to be skin and bones, didn't become one gram heavier. It wasn't like him to eat so much, either. For a long time he had been extremely choosy. Lots of uneaten food was cleaned out of his cage every day.

The strangest thing was that the food disappeared at night. As far as we knew Papen sat there and slept. He always went to sleep with his head under his wing.

One night when we stayed up longer than usual the mystery was solved. There was a rustling over in the cage. A mouse scurried around inside, eating a little of this and that, bustling and at home. Papen's cage was only cleaned in the morning, so the mouse was finding lots of things, leftovers from three human meals besides Papen's own food.

After a while the mouse, with a bite in her mouth, hopped over the serving table, darted down one of the cross legs and disappeared.

Not long after, she was up again to fetch a new bite. Papen wasn't sleeping. Papen understood perfectly what was going

on. With his head cocked, he looked with one eye down at the
mouse and found the whole thing very nice. He clucked softly
and contentedly.

We were so touched by the friendship that for some time
we didn't have the heart to intervene. But a mouse is a mouse;
you can't keep them for pets. It was clear that she had a nest
somewhere in the wall. The mouse was bringing food to her
young ones.

The hole was found, the trap set and the mouse family
caught in the trap. First the mother, then the many small baby
mice. They had an easy, quick death. There was no reason to
mourn them. But it hurt us for Papen's sake. Had it been
tolerably easy to find another parrot, I believe we would have
done it then. But it would have had to come all the way from
Oslo in that case. The idea was given up.

We consoled ourselves with the thought that there would
only be fighting, as peculiar and strange as Papen was. Birds
know as well as people who they like and who they don't, and
show it in a ruthless way. There was nothing to be gained by
flowing blood and flying feathers, we decided. But perhaps we
made a mistake in this, as in so many things.


When our home dissolved, Papen became even more
widely traveled. This time he took one of the express boats that
had finally replaced the old coastal steamer. He lived out his
last years at 12 Elisenbergveien in Oslo.

From that time on I saw him only at long intervals. My
aunts assured me he was lively and entertaining. Even so I had
the impression that for the most part he sat and slept, his eyes
covered by those strange lids, two white membranes that came
from above and below and met in the middle.

He was certainly tamer and nicer. He lived as well as a
lonely animal can, was the object of steady attention and may
well have become used to a little freedom, inasmuch as he died
in the sofa corner.

But he could have never lived really well. Papen's tragedy

was his loneliness. He should have had someone to fight with, if nothing else.


Papen lies buried in Ullernborg, outside Oslo. On the grave some small children, who knew him in his old age, have placed a white wooden cross.

# The Sisters

I T'S ONE of the days when Adele says it, says it again for the umpteenth time: She can't stand it any longer; she'll break down. Her hands hurt, her back hurts, she can't get any sleep on account of the pain; it makes her weep at night. She's not used to this kind of work, never will be, wasn't brought up for it, can't do it, doesn't want to do it, it will be the death of her. God only knows whether she's not already showing the signs – these sharp pains under her shoulder-blades....

She sits there with her bathrobe open over her pajamas, holding her cigarette in the way that frightens Tora, between her thumb and index finger, a bad sign. On good days she holds it between the index and middle fingers. Today....

Much is implied in that little gesture. Tora trembles when she sees it, doesn't dare look at Adele's face. She knows Adele will resemble an old roué. That sounds horrible, but it's true. She's got her eyes closed now and her lower lip pushed out and she's blowing smoke through her nostrils. She sits there like that terrible day in Copenhagen fifteen years ago. Tora will never forget it, the sad hotel room that looked out on to a narrow courtyard with high brick walls all around, the bottle of wine and the glass on the table, Adele's face and how she was dressed. Adele sat the way she does now, with her bathrobe open over her pajamas.

Tora remains standing there, small, gray, ordinary, buttoned straight up to the chin, ready to leave for work. She fingers the long horsehair necklace she always wears and quietly tries a little philosophy: If we mortals could teach ourselves to let every day take care of itself, to take it easy, not to hurry, not to demand the impossible, that everything be done right away. Adele really shouldn't take it so badly. Whatever doesn't get done today can be done tomorrow. They might get help, who knows? There's a lot of unemployment. Someone might pop up who'd gladly lend a helping hand for a reasonable wage – and be thankful for it....

But Adele knocks the ashes off her cigarette and says harshly, "The house costs us enough and more than enough as it is. We can't afford to have hired help. I work until my hands look like a ditch digger's." Adele thrusts her hands in front of Tora, shakes them in her face. "And still the house and the garden cost us ten thousand a year in upkeep. I am not exaggerating. The radishes cost us a krone apiece and the carrots two."

Tora is silent. She only looks upward a moment as if to call on heavenly assistance and says quietly, "We have a home here, Adele, let's remember that. We're on our own, don't owe anything to anybody. How would you like being in a big city apartment with thin walls, with phonographs and loudspeakers both above and below, with bedbugs maybe and with children right over your head. Let us be sincerely grateful..."

"When you start on gratefulness you're not far from God. Drag him out too while you're at it and thank him that you're alive and can move your arms and legs and aren't a cripple nor a poor feebleminded...."

Tora is silent again. Thank God that bad days pass. They come in cycles, one for every season. Now it's autumn, one of the worst times because of everything that has to be harvested from the garden. Tora submits, small, quiet and meek, but God knows it isn't easy. She has her work, her position at the local bank; she has to keep her head clear and her smile ready, be friendly to everyone and certain about where the dollar is, and the krone and the mark and the franc and the pound. Life is difficult. But it's given to us so we can learn from it, isn't it? Experience is what we reap – the only certainty – the only thing we know.

She puts on her coat and leaves. A little stoop-shouldered. Gray coat, gray hat, a small gray purse in her hand....

It's not easy, when you've been a traveling prima donna, when you've been acclaimed like Adele – stages full of flowers, storms of applause and curtain calls and bravos – a serenade by the Stavanger singing society – crowds in your dressing room between acts, champagne, letters, declarations – more flowers everywhere, all the way up to the towns in Finnmark where they're *very* expensive – like that time in Lillesand when she had to hire a man with a handcart to bring them back to the hotel...

It's not easy then to get up in the morning and dig for potatoes....

Adele – Good Lord, she was never with a major theater, never even with a resident company. A person doesn't always manage her talent in the best way; Adele certainly never has, she'd be the first to admit it. But in those places where she did appear, she was always number one, absolutely the number one prima donna. No one could have predicted that one day she'd be standing here digging up the earth.

If she says so herself – she had the looks. And the voice! "You have gold in your throat, child," her Danish singing teacher used to say when, as a young girl, she'd lived in Copenhagen to study music. And gold she'd had, an opera voice. If only she'd known how to take care of it. The temperament? My dear, she'd been sparkling, effervescent...

She'd believed in the future, in people, had a cheerful confidence in everything under the sun! Yes, that was then...

Her repertoire? Everything. From Violetta to Niniche. But there were no operas or operettas, no concert singing. She took a different path. Why? Because of a man, naturally. There's always a man behind it when a woman buries her talents. Adele has seen countless examples of it, not least in the theater. In order to forget a faithless man, in order to escape everything that reminded her of him, she had thrown her studies overboard and gone to join the Jørgensen company. The old story. You throw yourself into something new, thinking you can escape yourself, but you escape nothing... Not to criticize Jørgensen. He loved his art, lived for it, was an idealist. But he was obliged to play the Elf King in a knitted vest and gray wool socks. A gifted man like Nikolai Jørgensen. Don't tell me that life is anything but tragic. Mrs. Jørgensen? Ambrosia? A mother, a mother for Adele and the whole company. If you split your tights, presto, Ambrosia was there with needle and thread. If they didn't have the means to eat out one day, Ambrosia would collect her troops in the hotel room. You sat on the bed, on the trunks, on the table, on the window sills, held your knackwurst between two fingers and put your pint beer to your lips, in a brotherhood that was free as the wind. If you got a cold Ambrosia came along with a camphor rag, with warm milk and extra wool blankets when you'd gone to bed. It was like that with everything. When you think that she both directed and acted the most demanding roles — yes, those were the days, and you don't find people like the Jørgensens anymore.

Sometimes — months may go by but sometimes — Tora quietly interjects, "It sounded a little different in your letters to me at the time. You wrote about the miserable vagabond life, about trying to live on dry bread and biscuits because once again it had been impossible to get a penny of your pay, about the exploitative system, about..."

"Tora! I forbid you to speak in that manner. I don't want to hear it. You've never done anything but misunderstand. No one can say the least little thing to you without your distorting it. Good God, what do *I* need in order to live? Do I need a house with ten big rooms and a garden? Our grandfather had seven children, Tora, he built according to *his* need — but a bird of passage like me, used to being free and easy, coming and going as I please, I'm supposed to go around wearing myself to the bone just so we can ruin ourselves financially. You can say what you want, we are ruining ourselves, even though I go around from morning to night just like a maid. You sit in your

bank and think I'm lazy; you come home and everything is in
its place, food on the table, not a speck of dust. You console
yourself that I have Serine, but I'm telling you, Tora, it's not
within human power to manage everything here alone. We
work from morning to night, both she and I. I won't mention
the garden – I can't stand to talk anymore about it. And the
closed rooms. You think that all you have to do is close them
up, close them up and go away. But if we didn't air and wash
them from time to time, we'd be consumed by spiders and
vermin. An old house is an old house. Don't try to tell me that
we can rent rooms out, if you please. We couldn't handle having strangers with us, neither you nor I. No, if we're going to
do something, let's sell it. Why do we need all this? We could
be free as the breeze, we could travel. Just suppose you died
one day! Then I'd be alone in this out of the way place, forgotten by God and everyone. If it weren't that I didn't want to de-
sert you, leave you in the lurch...

"Do you live for free here? Because we own the house?
You're a child, Tora, you're living in a dream world. Ten
thousand in upkeep, not one penny less. Then there's the
ceilings to be whitewashed, and the stairs to be repaired, and
something's wrong with the chimney and the house leaks in
places when it rains, there's always something. Don't talk about
the home and the family estate, I know all that. I'll tell you
what you are, Tora, you're an egotist, an old egotist. You only
think about yourself and this blessed house. You don't give a
thought to my being buried alive here...."

Tora sighs. She doesn't try to contradict Adele again for
a long, long time.

When Tora comes home from the bank, she always takes
a swing by Petterson's grocery. Petterson has an unbelievably
good selection. She bends nearsightedly over Camembert and
Gorgonzola, carefully touches the French pears, browses along
the shelves, fetches small tin cans down with her own hands
and gives them to the cashier. "Wrap up this one, please, and

this one." Besides her bag, she always has a parcel or two. Outside the high, old-fashioned wooden fence she pauses a moment and listens. She has a peculiar, mouse-quiet manner, small and gray. Her whole life she's gone quietly around someone, listening and feeling her way. Around her parents first, then around her father, then around Adele. She has always listened for Adele, however, listened through letters, through their parents' worried lamentations, through her sister's own forced talkativeness when they met at rare intervals. The day the newspapers reported that Nikolai Jørgensen, who had widely traveled the Danish and Norwegian provinces for many years, was dead and that the company was on the verge of dissolving, Tora wrote immediately to Adele. When three weeks had passed without an answer, Tora went to Copenhagen.

Now she has this fixed place outside the wooden fence where she stands and listens and gets her bearings if she can.

If there's an aimless and absent-minded humming inside the garden, that's a good sign. If there's at the same time a light sound as of fine summer rain, Tora will smile, delighted. Now the flowers are being watered in the correct way, carefully, slowly. But if there is no humming; if, on the other hand, a strong splash breaks the silence, Tora trembles for her night-shade and her migonette. They don't recover, not for a long time, after such treatment.

If there's playing and singing indoors, it depends on what it is. The aria from *Tosca* doesn't bode well. It means intellectual restlessness, dissatisfaction, a troubled spirit. The Grand Duchess of Gerolstein is much better: "Tell him simply, our castle likes him/ Tell him simply, he's estee-emed/ Tell him simply, don't alarm him/ A lady's seen him and she's charmed." It suggests light resignation, a reconciliation with fate.

Niniche is the best. There are stanzas that make Tora's little gray face light up, make her go quickly and boldly in through the garden gate and call a cheery, "Hello, here I am!" under the open window. Above all it's this verse: "Oh, with a kiss, just a little one/ I avoided the cellblock and the whip/ If all judges were so lenient/ No one would ever go to prison."

Invariably after that follows an evening brimming over with gaiety, roses on the table, a great wave of old theater memories, champagne up from the cellar, a little teary melancholy when it begins to have an effect, and a kiss on the cheek and a "Thank you for the lovely evening, Tora." Then Tora is glad for the bottles she quietly brings home, to be scolded about if she's discovered with them. Then Adele holds her cigarette the way she's supposed to. Then Tora thinks, Everything blows over, everything turns out all right, if you just have patience. We'll stay in the house after all. One day we'll be put to rest here, one day we'll be carried out from here, thanks be to God.

She doesn't forget to thank Him in her evening prayers. She sleeps with a hint of triumph around her thin little mouth. Tora is one of those who wins in silence, that is to say, imperceptibly.

# Hval

THICKSET, red-faced, strapping as a farmer, gray felt hat pushed back on his head, cigar at the corner of his mouth, his heavy coat open, invariably wearing galoshes, and with a valise in one hand, he cleaves the crowd like a plow, moving in and out, putting down his name and an amount in the ledger over here, over there buying and selling right and left — the lord of the auction hall. The pawnbrokers' auction hall. Hval. Ola Hval. Grønlandsleret 16, door B off the entryway, fifth floor; gold of every alloy sold to dentists and jewelers. No auction takes place without him.

The gloomy old auction hall is his jungle, his hunting ground. He's well equipped with what the hunt demands: mental agility, quick reflexes, flair, perspective, fearlessness. Combined with a few other qualities that serve him well.

In his wake follow his henchmen, a gang of characters handy for almost anything: a rush errand, a prank, whatever is worth the effort. The wake is wide. Wherever Ola Hval goes first, two or three others can easily follow afterwards.

The hall is always crushingly full, especially in winter. There's the usual crowd that gathers whenever auctions are in progress and that follows bids and knockdowns as excitedly as the racing public follows galloping horses. There are all those who, homeless and jobless, need a place to hang around; this is what they've found. They stand clustered together far down the corridors, for it's both warm and entertaining here. There are the chance customers who come once and never again. Because they didn't do well; they got muddled and didn't buy

anything, or else they ended up with something they'd never
dreamed of. Then there are the lords of the marketplace, the
big-time buyers through whose hands goods pour in unbelievable quantities. Director Nathan, who just buys old family silver, an antique dealer, a middleman for antique dealers, a few
others. And Hval.

The further one pushes inside, the more tightly crammed
together the people are, and the more curiously complex the
air is. It reeks of both poverty and money's prerogative.
Money's prerogative can stink too. It can pay so little attention to
its outward appearance, be so completely absorbed in itself that
it becomes shabby and unkempt and goes around with a dirty
collar and black nails and a stale smell. Nathan doesn't, it's
true. Nor does Hval. He, in fact, has well-shined galoshes,
satin trimming on his topcoat and smokes a cigar. No one can
accuse him of slovenly opulence.

He makes his way through the crowd, inspects the pawned
goods, calls for things he inspected the other day, crams them
in his pocket or into his valise, studies his notes and makes new
ones, gives his troops orders, walks methodically and at the
same time quickly and resolutely forward. He finds time to
exchange a comradely word here and there, to shake hands, to
greet from a distance, with a raised right hand, another brother
in Mammon. Hval is a genial man, on a good footing with his
connections.

Gold is what he buys, gold of every alloy: watches, rings,
brooches, chains. He examines the stamp, weighs the object in
his hand, rejects or keeps it. If Hval keeps an object, it ceases
to have its own identity. It becomes meltable and usually looks
meltable, explain it who can. Only rarely does it retain a look
of value.

He goes home with his valise stuffed with gold and still
there's gold left over – gold he's bought but has had to leave behind to fetch the next day. It's said he does business throughout
the whole country, even in foreign countries: buying, melting
down and selling gold, gold, gold. He pays in hundreds, sometimes he pays in thousands. Or he hands over a lesser sum as

a deposit and brings the rest later. He can be trusted. An unceasing stream of gold runs through his fingers, the magical, mystical stuff from which power and glory and honor are created. Some people can't even manage to save a wedding ring out of this earthly life. Hval buys it, buys wedding rings by the handful, by the kilo, by the valise, and walks away with them. There's something fabulous about him, something all-consuming.

Naturally he's treated by everyone with great respect.

But one day someone calls out, "Hold on, Hval, just a moment!"

"Don't have time," Hval says. "Not now..."

"There's a lady here, Hval...."

"A lady?"

Hval casts an unwilling and suspicious sidelong look at the lady. He's short on time and has a notion of what it might concern. Yes, quite right, someone in reduced circumstances, modest to look at, who's out to buy back something or other, a pawn that came due and was sold and that she can't pay much for. He knows that sort, as do the others. "No time," says Hval, wanting to move on.

But the man who's made himself responsible for the lady, who's shown her the way and found Hval for her, persists, "It was you, wasn't it, Hval, who bought a ring and a chain the fifteenth of January, a gold chain and a diamond ring?"

"Don't remember," Hval declares. He gives the man, a buyer like himself, a look that as much as says, "What are you doing setting people on the trail of their securities? Just wait, I'll play you the same trick sometime. Sold is sold."

He wants to push his way past them, but more people have gathered, a couple of men from the offices where the books are kept. Around them people are craning their necks, not to see what's happening in the auction further inside but to look at Hval and the lady and her troop of helpers.

"Impossible to keep that kind of thing in your head," says Hval. "As much as I buy."

"It's recorded here, Hval. We have it in the books. You ran out of cash that day."

"That's right," comes from an outsider, who was there and remembers it well.

Hval looks around angrily and, at the same time, wonderingly. What do they mean, all of them? Does he act like this toward any of the others? No, no one could say that of him. It's obvious that everyone who saw the gold chain remembers it. It was such a piece of work that he himself, Ola Hval, was taken aback. He had wrapped it up by itself in tissue paper so it wouldn't get damaged among his other meltable goods. No harm in taking a closer look at it first. But what's bothering them? Is it sympathy for the lady? Once you start that, business goes to hell. She let the thing slip out of her hands and that's that. She's not a pretty girl either. Personally, that wouldn't have made any difference to him, but the whole business would be more understandable if she were. Now it's just badgering.

And damned if the bystanders don't start to discuss the chain, emphasizing its distinctive features. Someone maintains that it had small gold balls hanging from it; others think they weren't balls exactly, they were closer to small hearts.

"Hearts, yes!" the lady cries, clearly encouraged that so many remember it. "Small, small hearts, many small hearts...."

Hval thinks quickly. If it's a practical joke they want to play on him they're not going to find it so easy.

"Now I remember it," he says. "It's just dawned on me. I have the ring. You can have it back for thirty-five kroner."

"Thirty-five kroner," gasps the lady. "A diamond ring!"

"Thirty-five. That's cheap, but – far too cheap. Here's the address." He takes out and presents her with one of his printed cards: Ola Hval, Grønlandsleret 16, door B off the entryway. Like the precise businessman he is, straightforward and dependable in every way, he asks to have it back again a minute and adds in pencil the time of day he's most certain to be there – from five to seven. Then he wants to move on.

"But what about the chain?" says the lady.

"Melted down."

"That's not true," cries the lady loudly.

Hval looks around as if to call one and all to witness that here stands an irresponsible person accusing him, Ola Hval, of dishonesty. This, after having gotten back a diamond ring for thirty-five kroner.

"But that's murder!" cries the lady. "*Murder!*" And she continues saying that such things aren't done, it's unacceptable, it's barbaric, it's not possible, she can't believe it. She grabs Hval by the coat sleeve and shakes him.

At that there are faint smiles here and there. She got the ring at a bargain price, no one can say differently. Now she's hurting herself and throwing away sympathy.

Hval is on top again. Turning to everyone, and right over the lady's head, he assures them, "The chain was quite old-fashioned. It was worth the gold, nothing more. It's been sold for melting; it's only a lump now."

They nod to this all around. Whatever has become of the chain, Hval's been reasonable about the ring, he's been very good about the ring....

He plows on. Behind him he hears the lady: "It was a work of art, it didn't have anything to do with fashion. I don't believe it was destroyed, it's not possible."

A little circle of those who have nothing else to do continues to stand around her, trying to console her with the fact that at least she got the ring cheap, she must be glad about that.

She turns up at Hval's in the afternoon; she comes up the dark stairs, peers at the names on the doors in the vanishing gleam of a skylight, and rings. An indolent female in a dressing gown opens the door part-way.

Is Hval home? The indolent woman sucks her teeth instead of answering, goes off, sucking her teeth, through another door, and the lady is led in.

Hval sits at a large table in the middle of the room. There

is gold on the table, gold in piles, rings especially, wedding rings, hundreds of them, perhaps thousands. The room has windows on two sides. The mound of gold on the table catches both the glow of the evening sky outside and the electric bulb that hangs from the ceiling; it throws its brilliance from right to left and up again, shining in the double light like a barbaric idol. The top of Hval's head shines too, but with a more subdued light. Otherwise everything lies in deathly shadow.

Hval is sorting. He's made some smaller gold mounds around the large one. He grasps each ring, holds it up to the lightbulb, examines the stamp and puts it down. The lady has to stand waiting. She stares at the gold.

"Yes, well then," says Hval. "About that ring." He pulls out a drawer full of boxes and bags and, out of one of the bags, the lady's ring. It's the right one, neither of them is in doubt about that. He hasn't exchanged it for another; there's no such difficulty.

"Thirty-five kroner, if you please. It's far too cheap, but – you can be glad it was me you had to deal with. I laid the ring aside for the sake of the stone. Many people would have knocked out the stone, of course, and melted down the ring. And now I'm being as reasonable as I can."

He is sorting again, intensely occupied as always.

"Thank you very much," says the lady. She places the money on the table, takes the ring and remains standing.

She begins to unwrap something she carries under her arm, a large photograph framed and behind glass, a picture of herself when she was younger, with the necklace around ner throat. Pretty, as a matter of fact. A young woman in full bloom, with wavy blond hair, sweet bare arms and high delicate breasts in a ballgown, the kind that was in fashion eighteen or twenty years ago. It's unbelievable but true – the faded lady and the lady in the picture are one and the same person.

"See here." The lady puts her finger on the necklace, which is particularly prominent.

"Yes, I see, I recognize it well. That was the one, I see it all right." Hval allows himself a moment for a sidelong glance at the portrait, though he has other things to do.

The lady comes closer with the picture, holds it in front of his face. "Are you sure? Can it be possible? I mean, for..."

"To change the subject," says Hval. "You won't forget to go back to the pawnshop with the receipt and get the balance refunded, will you? The balance is yours, don't forget. Many people do..."

"Of course you weren't intending to sell it," says the lady stupidly, completely idiotically.

And since she starts in again with "she can't believe," etc., Hval has to take the time for a longer explanation; he first went to Afaneff with the necklace. She knows Afaneff, who takes all kinds of jewelry on commission. Since it really was a very pretty necklace Hval wanted to see what he could get for it. Afaneff didn't even want it. No one was looking for that sort of thing anymore. The only thing left was to melt it down.

With that he inspects in great detail a ring he has between his fingers. When he looks up again the lady is finally gone.

He shrugs his shoulders. To the indolent woman, who indolently appears in the doorway, he says, "Talk about demanding. She got the ring back for thirty-five kroner, got it as a present really. But does she leave it at that? Hardly. I told her again it had been melted down, that's what I told her...."

The indolent woman smiles from one corner of her mouth; she shrugs her shoulders as well and sucks her teeth. She comes over to the table, stands there with one hand on her hip and with the other hand collects five wedding rings. She spreads them out in front of her and indolently plays jacks with them. Her position is such that she can do that.

The day after, Hval is plowing his usual way through the crowd. Hat pushed back on his head, top coat open, galoshes, cigar. And damned if the lady isn't there again!

She follows in his wake, surfaces near him, and says loudly, "You were definitely not at Afaneff's with the necklace. Afaneff has never seen it before. I showed him the photograph

and he said that kind of workmanship is never melted down.
Tell me now what it will cost to get it back. At least let me
know what you want."

And before he knows it, a crowd gathers again. There are
enough people here just standing around waiting for something
to happen. They draw close together, eyes alert with excitement. Someone from the business office is there like the previous time, following everything attentively; he has time for this
in the middle of business hours. He's pushed this way and that
by the crowd, but keeps his place and looks sharply at Hval,
stands there staring. There are a couple of buyers as well. . . .

Hval looks around, as if he were thinking, Is this the end
of solidarity here? Is it war?

He tosses his head and wants to plow onward.

"Listen here, Hval," says the man from the business office.
"Is it true that. . . ?"

There's something in the air, something uncertain and
irritating that suddenly makes Hval angry. He doesn't express
it and he doesn't show it; he stands there, to all appearances
calm, confident in the knowledge that he's bought and paid for
the necklace. The rest concerns no one as long as law and order
reign in the land. They won't get far with slander, though it's
best to keep the peace as long as possible. He offers a brief
explanation, "It's true, all right. Bought is bought and melted
is melted."

Silence.

"Afaneff," cries the lady.

"I never mentioned Afaneff," says Hval. He can safely say
that. There wasn't a hint of a witness to any such mention. He
stems the tide of the mass of people with his shoulder and
plows off for good. The lady remains behind with her mouth
open, and he hears her crying out about murder and lies, hears
them calming her. A little later, when he's on his way out, she's
gone. But damned if they don't keep staring anyway, all those
hangers-on.

Hval considers a moment. It's not something he often does,

not publicly anyway. He's fast, uninterrupted action personi-
fied. He gives one of his henchmen a few short orders, leaves
the hall in the middle of business hours, to the general consternation of the crowd, and is gone the rest of the morning. An
idea came as if tossed to him. If they harass him, he'll harass
them, the whole bunch of them, without fear or favor. Something odd has been in the air since yesterday. He can't quite
make it out, but now that he thinks about it, it might not be
the first time he's felt it.

There'd better not be anything in the air here. Nothing
whatsoever. If they don't know who he is yet, they soon will.


He turns up punctually for the big afternoon auction of
over twelve hundred lots of gold and silver pledges.

His valise gives the impression of remarkable heaviness,
almost as if he were on his way from an auction and not to one.
Something also goes on inside it, when he puts it down, a kind
of weighty clinking.

But people have other things to think about; those who notice it soon forget it again. It's an exciting auction, one that has
to do with objects of considerable worth, and the buyers have
been sounding each other out in the exhibit room for many
days. The appropriate mood of tense excitement is soon evi-
dent, and the auctioneer ably stirs it up. This is going to be a
long one, in any case.

Hval stands as usual in the first row — red-faced, strapping, watchful, notes in hand, bidding as usual against the
other buyers. More casual customers who want to keep up stay
on as long as Hval and his associates want them to, no longer.

The objects go in lots. Just the way they once were wrapped
up, carried off and pawned. Single wedding rings, two wedding rings tied together, with some teaspoons or perhaps a
watch. Vainglorious jewelry that has ended up here because it
simply cost too much, and modest pieces that couldn't be res-
cued, even though they're worth almost nothing in cash. Fam-

ily heirlooms and glittering *funkisprakt** and chalices and coffee services and goblets with inscriptions and forks and even gold-rimmed spectacles.

Hval's first purchase is a diverse lot — rings and bracelets, rather solid things. It's up to two hundred seventy kroner when the hammer falls. "Cash or on the books?" asks the auctioneer and prepares to write. "Cash," says Hval, bending down and opening up his valise. Clearly he intends to pack the things away immediately.

But instead Hval takes money out of the valise, thick bundles of notes, and begins to count them out. "Don't you have any larger bills?" the clerk asks when he sees they're just five-kroner notes. "No," says Hval, wetting his thumb and counting out a new bundle. "Here you are, you may count it," he says and hands a huge pile of five-kroner notes across the table. "Here's two hundred forty-five for now."

He bends down again and brings out of the valise large numbers of one-kroner coins, twenty of them; then he begins on the ten øres, in even greater numbers, forty of them. He places them all together in small stacks all over the table. "Here's some, here's some more."

"Now listen, Hval, if this is your idea of being funny, then..."

"Twenty-one, twenty-two, twenty-three," says Hval, who is now counting out one-øre pieces, counting and counting until it becomes clear to the crowd that the last of the sum will be paid in this denomination.

"But seriously, Hval, if everyone came and paid in this way..."

"Let them," says Hval. "According to the regulations, no more than twenty can be paid in single kroners, no more than five in smaller coins and no more than one in copper. Larger sums in notes. So this should be all right. Go ahead, you can't refuse money from the national mint." He keeps on shoving the

---

*Swedish functional ware, first displayed at the Stockholm Exhibition in 1930. – Trans.

money over to the clerk who counts it with sweat on his brow, while the whole auction stands still. Hval nudges his valise slightly with his foot. It clinks ominously.

"Yes, well, well, it wasn't a bad joke. But now let's get on with things. If you buy more today we'll put your name down as usual; you can use some of your fivers to make deposits..."

"My name will never appear in the books here again," says Hval and puts his fist down hard on the table. "I've had more than enough inconvenience from that. Anyway, you can't say anything against people who pay cash, can you?"

He stands there broad and immovable, chewing on his cigar and looking around challengingly. And he slings out recklessly, "Go on, why don't you?"

"Throw 'im out," someone shouts.

Hval doesn't even turn his head.

The auctioneer bites his lip, but doesn't say anything. Turned to the crowd, he's caught the expressions of several faces, the elbowings here and there. The news of Hval's new manner of paying has already spread, leaking everywhere, even reaching the other room — it's obvious from various signs. It might be difficult for the hand of the law to strike Hval down if he perseveres, but there are other hands — Fate's, you might say.

The auctioneer brings another pair of lots forward. Small lots. Hval chews on his cigar and allows them, after a tense moment, to go by. Then a large lot comes along. Hval bids; Hval has it knocked down to him.

The excitement is great now. There's a wave of craning necks, lifted heads, shoulders and elbows bumping each other. A great deal smoulders among those who are gathered here: simple curiosity, the normal human hope of a spectacle of some kind, but also of something suppressed and dangerous. More than one has seen his things — things that were symbols and gave life a framework and solidity — disappear into Hval's valise, become goods to be melted down and taken away. And has felt it as a burning injustice. More than one has also held back angry words when Hval, with marvelous cold-blooded-

ness, helped himself to a tasty morsel. Perhaps, when it comes
down to it, he's not on such a good footing with his connections
as is believed.

This time it's over three hundred kroner. Hval has to pay
up. He lets the valise stand completely open on the floor in
front of him, so there's a clear view of what's inside it. It's full
of money, in bundles, in coinrolls. He can keep this situation
going forever. He counts, the clerk counts; it will never end.
The auctioneer looks out over the gathering; the other buyers
turn and do the same. Whether there is an appeal in this or not,
a certain element understands it as such.

The crowd is strangely, quietly in motion. There's pushing
here and there, nodding and winking.

Up in front Hval is counting, arranging bundles and
stacks, shoving them over the table to the clerk. The clerk is
counting....

It was probably around half past three when Hval was
thrown out the window. Was carried over to it and heaved outside. Later he claimed that a signal was given to the perpetra-
tors, by those he least expected it from. But that was, of course,
impossible to prove. There was, on the whole, not much to
prove. For in the end it was as if everyone, high and low, was
in on this together.

It was a first floor window, so Hval didn't break anything.
But he was certainly a little stiff and lame when he got up to
go. Very dirty too, for there was frost on the bare ground. His
felt hat had fallen off and had lost its shape. Hval had to stand
there, in front of everyone, knock the dirt off it and put the
dent back in the top. This was done with a resolute thump of
his right hand. He didn't lose his outward calm for a moment,
not even when he received a quick blow in the back from someone's cane. His valise was also heaved out, was passed down
and placed at his side. After he managed to brush himself off
a little and had his hat on again, he picked it up. Then the police
came; someone had secretly alerted them.

Everything depends on how you take it.

The one eventually charged and fined was Hval himself, even though he had the law on his side. He was charged with inciting a riot.

But besides quickness and flair he has some other useful traits. He's himself again. He plows through the crowd as before and hasn't diminished an inch. Blocking his intentions is something no one does anymore. And that can be worth a fine.

When he, for the first time after the incident, let them write down an amount for him, it was a kind of historic moment. He stood supporting himself with one clenched hand on the table. He said, "Write it down!" He lifted his head at the same time, looked around at those present, cleared his throat audibly, straightened up, put both hands behind his back and remained standing like that.

# A Mystery

SHE ARRIVED in a terrible storm. It didn't look odd in the least not to go on board, so Mrs. Isaksen didn't, but kept in the lee of merchant Flåten's warehouse on the wharf; she stood there wearing Isaksen's sou'wester and raincoat and looked on, while a solitary passenger came up on deck and fought her way down the gangway. There was no doubt who the passenger was.

Mrs. Isaksen didn't go to meet her, but turned in the opposite direction toward Kaia, who sat in Ola Galterud's cart under the maples by the telegraph station, called out something about the horse, about being sure to hold him well, in case the steamer should blow. The words were carried off in the gale, and Mrs. Isaksen added loudly to herself that she had misgivings and that she was annoyed Kaia hadn't heard her.

In this way the stranger came unnoticed right up behind the warehouse. There she stopped and said, "Is this Mrs. Isaksen?" And the wind bore it along, so you couldn't possibly avoid hearing it. Mrs. Isaksen started in surprise, turned and shouted with all her might — she had both the head wind and something else to overcome — "Hello, hello, welcome. This must be Mrs. Arnold."

"Yes, I am. I'm so grateful to you that I could come."

"Oh, my dear...."

Mrs. Isaksen stopped. It was only right that Mrs. Arnold be grateful. She certainly had reason to be. On the other hand there was no need for effusiveness. That kind of thing could easily get out of hand. It was just as well that Mrs. Isaksen made her own position clear, now as later, by shouting, "It's for Uncle's sake..."

"Of course, I understand that," said Mrs. Arnold, growing red. She turned to the man with the baggage. And Mrs. Isaksen, who saw her now from the back, ascertained in silence: Beautiful coat, good shoes, pretty hat — looks anything but needy — I can't offer her my old gray coat after all....

The gale put a temporary stop to all conversation. It was all she could do to shout that, yes, it was that cart up there. Nonetheless Mrs. Isaksen shouted an additional, "Horrible weather." To be friendly and to make it clear she was a kind, courteous, easy-to-get-along-with person. Up by the cart she shouted, in addition, "My daughter, Kaia," pointing up at the seat. Kaia raised herself slightly, producing with bent knees something between a nod and a curtsey, neither one nor the other and a little of each.

They drove off. Out on the main road the gale winds increased, swept howling over them, allowing no conversation. All the same, in her role of hostess, Mrs. Isaksen shouted one thing or another with all her strength: "The minister lives there!" "There's the farm where we get our milk." "This cart is rented from there." "Summer visitors are everywhere!" "We live around that bend over there!"

Mrs. Arnold nodded in appreciative surprise at every announcement and said, "Really?" She looked frozen and worn out, and it was difficult to decide how her pale blue face looked under normal conditions. Her teeth were chattering. Mrs. Isaksen thought, Do I have to offer her anything before supper? She could easily get the idea that we're well off. I think I'll leave it be. Hmmm, no, I've got to offer her a cup of tea anyway.

"I hope you'll be content with how we live," she shouted then. "We rent out one floor in the summer, as you know. We have to, unfortunately. A folding cot in the dining room is all I have to offer you."

"Thank you very much," shouted Mrs. Arnold. "Just your taking me in is so kind."

"For Uncle's sake!" emphasized Mrs. Isaksen once more

so that she definitely couldn't be accused of contributing to any misunderstanding herself. Then they rolled up to the house.

On the porch Isaksen stood with a pipe and in slippers. He looked almost animated and, in spite of his slippers, descended a few steps to greet the guest.

"A hearty welcome!" he called, but got a look from his wife, and welcomed her again in a way that was correct, nothing more.

In the doorway off the entry hall Mrs. Isaksen stopped and turned to her husband. Inside the room she saw a table set with cups and saucers and quite a few things to eat.

"I thought you might be cold after the drive so I asked Andrine to make some coffee," Isaksen explained.

"Coffee?" Mrs. Isaksen's face went stiff. The price of cream went up yesterday, she thought. If Yngve comes home before supper there'll be five of us besides Andrine. We live like every day were our last. Aloud she said, "A cup of tea would have suited us better."

But Isaksen was silently examining Mrs. Arnold, who had taken off her outer garments now and stood there smoothing her hair, slender and neat and with something about her that you didn't see among the women in his house. A bit the worse for wear, all right. But not too bad really, all things considered. Frankly he'd imagined her differently, with a little more of a — well, frivolous — character. But now, watching her, he was interested and not unsympathetic. Married and divorced and married again down in Germany. And now escaping from husband number two. Good God, yes, that could naturally mean, as his wife maintained, that Mrs. Arnold was probably quite an impossible person. From the beginning he'd agreed that there was no reason in the world to make changes in the daily routine for the sake of this unknown and slightly obscure woman, whom he'd met on the stairs in his slippers. Now he felt uncomfortable and regretted the slippers; he was almost inclined to believe that it was the two gentlemen something was wrong with. She really did look like a pretty, refined lady.

He engaged the guest in conversation. Isaksen had been

in Berlin a couple of years ago; he could talk about lots of things — about his hotel, streetlife, prices, the joys and discomforts of travel; Danish, German, Swedish and Norwegian customs officials. To be honest, he himself had tried a little smuggling too, had a good many more cigarettes than was allowed on his return, besides other small things. And there'd been no problem. Apropos of cigarettes, however — did Mrs. Arnold smoke? He himself valued a good pipe far more, but he did have a few on hand. He got up and brought them out.

Mrs. Arnold warmed up and got some color in her face, whether it was because of the coffee or because of Isaksen. She answered cheerfully, lit a cigarette, blew a ring....

Under the circumstances Mrs. Isaksen found it best to bring the pair back to earth again. She said, "I'll unfortunately have to ask you to be on your feet a little early in the morning, Mrs. Arnold, so the maid can come in to air the room and so on before breakfast..."

Mrs. Arnold reddened again. Lord only knew if she weren't a little touchy and easily wounded, one of those you can't say a word to. But she answered politely that she hoped she wouldn't oversleep; she didn't, as a rule. For that matter she slept by an open window and she'd naturally make the cot and fold it up herself...

"Yes, thank you very much for doing it," came coldly from Mrs. Isaksen. "We'll put in a wash basin, then, on a chair. As I've mentioned, it's a little primitive at our house in summer." She thought, Aha, maybe you're one of those terribly modest and helpful people, who think they acquit themselves so well that they can just stay and stay. This is where one should be on one's guard, all right....

The next morning Mrs. Arnold got coffee in bed. That wasn't being on one's guard; it was far beyond what one was obliged to do. But it was part of the family tradition and it was impossible to disregard the guest, especially since she slept next to the kitchen. Andrine had orders to put *one* slice of white bread, no more, on the *saucer* next to the cup and spoon. And two lumps of sugar. So it was completely clear that this was an incentive to get up, nothing else; certainly it was no meal to lie there lingering over. Andrine did as she was told. And Mrs. Arnold got up.

And the days began to pass. Already in the course of the first day, Yngve, who had been polite and respectful the evening before, listening to the adults' conversation, had become totally himself again, interrupting them, snorting at what they said, slurping loudly, reaching over the table for food, helping himself so that Mrs. Isaksen felt herself forced to clear her throat. Under other circumstances she would have tried to hold him in check a bit in front of company, given him a little kick under the table anyway. Now she let it pass, true to her plan: no changes in their daily life, no extra arrangements.

In many ways Mrs. Arnold was irreproachable. She got up early, offered to help with one thing or another, took modest helpings at the table, wrote and also received letters, remained in contact with the outside world. There was hope that something was happening, that not everything rested solely on the Isaksens.

For the rest she looked after herself, took long walks in the woods and didn't demand to be entertained.

But —

Could reserve be carried too far? Mrs. Isaksen wouldn't ask, not for anything in the world. It was so easy to get on intimate terms; it would just make this person feel far too much at home.

On the other hand you'd think it wasn't totally unreasonable to expect Mrs. Arnold herself to have something to say about her situation and her plans. So you'd have *something* to go by.

"For a short while," Uncle wrote. Could his deceased friend's only daughter stay with them for a short while? Until she could get herself straightened out and get on her feet again? She'd been living in unhappy circumstances down in Germany, but had left now and for the moment was poverty stricken and alone in the world. Mrs. Isaksen, as a woman, could understand and help her better than he could. She would do her old uncle a great favor.

Mrs. Isaksen definitely wanted to do her uncle a great favor. He was a widower, childless, well off and close to eighty. He could have taken Mrs. Arnold in himself, but he probably didn't dare because of his housekeeper; Lina wouldn't allow it so he seized on this idea.

Mrs. Isaksen opened her home, was willing to do it, yes, even to share her wardrobe if it came down to it. She wasn't inhuman. But she liked a situation to be clear and straightforward. And the one she found herself in was not only unclear, it was oppressive.

A short while, what did that mean? Was it a week or was it a year? And what was Mrs. Arnold doing about finding herself a livelihood? Was she doing anything at all about it? She hadn't inquired, verbally at any rate, about possibilities in the neighborhood or in the nearest town. It wasn't unreasonable to expect that. She sent and received letters. And Lord knows what *they* had in them. If it weren't that you could see her sitting and writing at the dining table with slashed-open letters bearing Norwegian and German stamps in front of her, you'd wonder about her whole correspondence. For Mrs. Arnold didn't collect her letters at merchant Flåten's like everyone else; she went to meet the postman – every single day, Isaksen, *every* day, long trips – talk about suspicious natures.

And that Mr. Arnold – was he brutal? Did he drink? Had he been unfaithful? Surely there had to be serious grounds for a person just to up and leave a husband and throw herself on strangers. Unless the party concerned was exceptionally pushy and demanding. One or the other, admit it, Isaksen.

Isaksen admitted a great deal, little by little. His sympathy was decreasing; it had been put to the test.

Under the pretext that otherwise the guest could easily get the notion they were well off, Mrs. Isaksen had from the first moment introduced fare that, without exaggeration, could be called spartan. All the cheese and cold cuts vanished, with the exception of brown goat cheese. That remained as always by Mrs. Isaksen's place, and as always she cut thin slices of it, easing it on to the plates. But she didn't offer seconds even to her husband. And she remained completely oblivious to signs from any other quarter.

Isaksen's pint of beer had disappeared. Coffee after dinner had disappeared. If anyone alluded to the fact that these were major changes in the daily routine, Mrs. Isaksen said, "Shhhh!"

On the eighth day Yngve said, out in the hall, so loudly that it was heard clearly inside, "If she doesn't move on soon, I'll do something or other, put itching powder in her bed or something...."

There wasn't just a steamer to the nearest town; there was a bus too. Isaksen took the bus every morning, disappearing for the rest of the day. He had an office there and business affairs, wholesaling something indeterminate.

Mrs. Arnold didn't sit down then with needlework, like Mrs. Isaksen and Kaia and the summer guests upstairs, an older woman and two daughters who were in the habit of calling "Good morning" from the balcony and liked coming down and sitting on the steps with their sewing things. They had been summer guests at the Isaksens for many years – they took good care of the furniture and properly replaced anything that got broken. The relationship was the best possible.

Mrs. Arnold didn't have any sewing things; she didn't even have any clothes that needed mending or putting in order – only new, whole things. A poverty-stricken woman! Understand that if you could.

She helped out with the daily chores, dusting and watering flowers; she would gladly take a dish of peas out of Andrine's hands and start shelling them. She asked if there were errands to run and ran them. But if it involved putting a new patch on Yngve's trousers, just to take a small example, she never offered her help. She vanished into the woods.

The day she sat down and darned some of her own stock-

ings, Mrs. Isaksen actually breathed a sigh of relief and almost
fell into spontaneous amiability. Now Mrs. Arnold was showing a normal side, a sort of justification for living. But when
the stockings were darned, they were darned. Mrs. Arnold
rushed off to the woods again and compromised the Isaksens
just as much as before.

Compromising – that was it precisely. It wasn't possible
to ignore it any longer; that was what she was, this lady who
wandered around on roads where no one else went, hoarding
her letters to herself instead of crowding with the rest around
the postman outside Flåten's at one o'clock, calling, "Anything
for me, Karlsen?" Who swam when the beach was empty and
deserted and, in other words, kept herself apart. People were
wondering. Mrs. Isaksen and Kaia were well aware of it. Little
by little they were closely questioned both by the ladies upstairs and as they stood waiting their turn in the shop. "You
have a guest, I see? A relative? Oh, isn't she? A married
woman, I hear? Can she just be away from home like this?
Maybe she needed to be away a while to rest – that's what a lot
of people need to do, though of course not everyone can, unfortunately. No children? Well now, that's a different story."

And so forth –

Most people would have probably ignored it, thought up
something or other, but Mrs. Isaksen wasn't talented that way;
she wasn't the sort that *can* lie, she didn't have that gift. When
she said briefly that it was a daughter of one of her uncle's old
friends, people looked as if they imagined all sorts of things. If
only she could have expanded upon the sufferings Mrs. Arnold
had been through – but there she stood. And Mrs. Arnold
went around well dressed, polite and correct, didn't look desti-
tute or weighed down with grief, and didn't even sit sewing.

Mrs. Isaksen couldn't get any of it to add up. She was
turning into a nervous wreck from it, began to lie awake at
night.


Lord knew what Mrs. Arnold was doing on her walks. She

could be gone for hours on end. Returning home she often brought something or other – edible mushrooms, berries, flowers. Mrs. Isaksen would have appreciated this, if it weren't for the nagging thought that perhaps Mrs. Arnold believed that she was contributing something and that now she could just stay and stay.

Then, one day, Kaia came running in, out of breath. She'd seen Mrs. Arnold sitting on a stump in the woods, crying.

"What are you saying? Where? When?"

"A little while ago. In the north woods."

"And she didn't see you?"

"Oh no." Kaia had walked on just the moss and had stood hiding behind the trees.

"Are you sure she was crying?"

"*Crying!* She was bawling."

Mrs. Isaksen sat silent a while, thinking intently. "Hmmm," she said. "So now we're going to have scenes, on top of everything else. How did we get involved in this! But thank you very much, Kaia. I'm glad you came and told me about it, dear."

When Mrs. Arnold arrived for dinner an hour later a certain excitement manifested itself in the Isaksen family. Yet she didn't look either red-eyed or sorrowful; on the contrary, she was livelier and more communicative than ever before.

Then she disappeared again for an evening walk. Mrs. Isaksen sat there, with her hands in her lap, sighing again over what she'd sighed over many times before, "She's a mystery to me. A complete mystery."

One day Kaia came to report that Mrs. Arnold was sitting on a stone now, wiping her eyes and eating *pâté*.

"*Pâté!*" Mrs. Isaksen bounded from her chair. "Are you completely crazy?"

Kaia wasn't one bit crazy; she'd seen it on the tin, one of the oval ones with gold print like Flåten had in his window. It was on the ground along with a package of biscuits. And as she was saying, Mrs. Arnold sat on a stone, spreading *pâté* on the biscuits with a little pocketknife and eating amazingly fast, either because she was so hungry or because she had to eat it up right away. Sometimes she took her handkerchief out and wiped her eyes.

"I'm totally at sea," said Mrs. Isaksen. "It's shameful. Instead of coming and asking for a sandwich. If anyone sees her, they'll think she doesn't get fed here. But, of course, *pâté* isn't served in this house..."

"No, that's for sure," said Kaia. "But that's nothing to her; she just goes and buys it herself...."

After that, with lips pressed together, Mrs. Isaksen went inside to bring out the snack of white bread and juice that she had recently, when the family was alone, been offering as a sacrifice to domestic opinion.

That afternoon Mrs. Arnold even wanted to tell them a story. But she didn't get very far.

Yngve was digging in a flowerpot with one finger when she came in. And see if she didn't light into him and jerk his hand out of the pot, saying, "But you've got an open cut there...."

"Yeah, so what?" snorted Yngve.

"There can be dangerous bacteria in the earth," said Mrs. Arnold. "Tetanus," she said. "Go and put some iodine on it right away."

Yngve snorted even more. "That's stupid, iodine on a scratch."

"Small wound, needy friends," said Mrs. Arnold. And she began to tell her story, began eagerly and rather quickly.

She knew of a case down in Germany: It was a singer, in fact, who was going to sing at a funeral. He'd looked a little peculiar right before, had admitted that he didn't feel well. But he didn't want to cancel. And so — in the middle of the song — he suddenly couldn't move his lower jaw — his mouth stayed open, paralyzed. He died a few hours later in great suffering — and it came out, it came out — that that same day — he'd been planting roses — he was a flower-lover — he'd had a tiny little cut no one would bother about — a barely visible cut on his finger.

Mrs. Arnold couldn't go on from here. It was as if her own lower jaw also stiffened up in a cramp. There's something tragic about an audience that doesn't give a single sign it's listening and taking it in. That, on the contrary, suddenly exchanges loud remarks on quite different subjects, in this case, a spool of white thread.

"Oh, hand me that white spool, Kaia, I see I have to fasten those buttons better," was what Mrs. Isaksen said.

"Here you go," said Kaia.

"Thanks very much, dear, here you go. Don't forget to buy another number forty when you go to Flåten's," said Mrs. Isaksen.

After that it was completely quiet for a while.

"I'm sorry. Weren't you telling us something or other, Mrs. Arnold?" Mrs. Isaksen looked up distractedly from her sewing.

"Me? Oh, no."

"Imagine. I thought you were...."

Right afterwards Mrs. Arnold disappeared. She probably went out for a walk again.

Mrs. Isaksen shrugged her shoulders. "Good Lord, we're really able to deal with our scratches ourselves," she said. "Come here, boy, let me have a look at you...."


It became known that Mrs. Arnold consumed, in turn, crab, chocolate and cheese in the woods. The Isaksen family, which for her sake had imposed privation and self-denial on itself, became bitter. It smouldered dangerously in a couple of quarters. Both Yngve and Kaia made remarks frequently under their breath. Isaksen took it more calmly. He wasn't in town for nothing every single day; he knew where to find the best hot sandwiches. One day — it was the thirteenth — fish balls were reported. The way they came, out of the can, cold. But Mrs. Arnold couldn't handle them. After she'd eaten three, she shuddered as if nauseated, sighed and buried the can and its contents in the moss. Kaia could point out the place where it happened, was ready to do it right away if necessary. Mrs. Arnold was sure not to return for a long time; she'd disappeared into the woods. Yngve could come along.

Yngve came along.

A couple of hours later when Mrs. Arnold opened the gate, the can of fish balls stood in the middle of the yard. The widow upstairs opened her window at the same time and called down in surprise, "Look, there's practically a full can of fish balls right in the middle of the yard. You think Andrine's forgotten them? Well, I only want to warn you — there are cats around — humph — I almost think it looks like they've been here already."

Mrs. Arnold stopped, turned blood red. But it passed quickly and she said calmly, yes, even with a little smile, "Maybe Yngve and Kaia know something about it. They're standing in back of the door, both of them."

She walked past the can, past them and past Mrs. Isaksen ... who, uneasy, had appeared in a doorway further inside. She took a book and sat down. With a smile!

But that evening there was fried whiting for supper at the Isaksens, explain it who can. Mrs. Isaksen made an attempt by saying, "Ola Galterud came by with some fresh fish. I felt I had to take it — a little taste of something is good with the bread now and then."

No one contradicted her. Isaksen boldly ordered a bottle of beer and offered the ladies some.


Two days later Mrs. Arnold came in with a letter in her hand and announced that she was leaving on the night boat.

"And now I must thank you sincerely for the wonderful hospitality you've shown me," she said.

It came as a complete surprise to Mrs. Isaksen; she broke out, flabbergasted, "But my dear, you're leaving? Are things working out a bit for you then? I thought..."

Mrs. Arnold interrupted her, lightly and confidently, "Yes, thank you. I can imagine you'll be glad to get rid of me.

I've taken advantage of your kindness far too long."

"My dear, it's been a pleasure. When you're willing to take things the way they are here," she said unexpectedly and thoughtlessly. To tell the truth, she lost her composure for a moment. But it came back again; she called out to Andrine to put Mrs. Arnold's bedclothes out to air, immediately, so they'd get the benefit of the sun while it was out – Mrs. Arnold was leaving this very day.

That makes it a little more certain that it will really happen, thought Mrs. Isaksen, with the idea of cutting off her retreat. Within moments Andrine came out dragging the pillows and blankets.

Mrs. Arnold went in to pack.

They drove to the wharf in Ola Galterud's wagon. Mrs. Arnold wanted to pay for it herself, but Mr. and Mrs. Isaksen assured her in unison that no, there couldn't be any talk of that. Mrs. Arnold had to give way and say, thank you very much, it was far too much.

She didn't say a word about where she was going. She talked quickly and animatedly about anything and everything, about weather and wind, but she also withdrew into herself for moments at a time and sat looking, preoccupied, out over the landscape. More than once Mrs. Isaksen had a question on her lips, but it wasn't exactly easy to get out, though it was basically a simple thing to ask. Anyway, Mrs. Arnold kept circumventing her by her constant talk of other things. Finally it was Isaksen who asked. And then Mrs. Arnold answered with a wistful smile, a shrug of the shoulders, a gesture that hinted that the wide, but cold world lay open to her: "Traveling on."

And there sat the Isaksens.

"Well, I was actually thinking of the mail; more letters could come that need forwarding," Isaksen mumbled feebly.

"Yes, letters, yes." Mrs. Isaksen entertained new hope.

But Mrs. Arnold assured them calmly and cheerfully that no more letters would come.

It was a still evening, warm and clear with a softly gurgling sea, blue hills, reddening sky. On board it looked inviting and

comfortable, with travelers in folding chairs on the deck and
the lights on in the salon. Mrs. Arnold tripped over the gang-
plank in her pretty coat and was a completely different person
than when she arrived – a travelwise lady of the continental cut
who was traveling in earnest, no one knew how far, a true
globetrotter. She commanded respect, no more, no less.

She decidedly declined Isaksen's offer to see to a berth immediately; she wouldn't even hear talk of him carrying her baggage down below. "We'll chat and have a nice time together as
long as we can," she said, taking her things out of his hands
and setting them down in the smoking cabin. "I'm sure I'll get
a berth."

And she chatted. Now, for the first time, it became apparent how winning, lively and amusing Mrs. Arnold could be.
She spoke cheerfully and effortlessly on the beauty of the
place, the beauty of the evening, the difference between the
German and Norwegian landscape, the character of the German and Norwegian peoples. She said one striking thing after
another. And the Isaksen family came to feel stranger and
stranger, more and more crestfallen. Especially when, in the
middle of everything else, she assured them that she couldn't
thank them enough.

Good Lord, if they'd only known before that she hadn't
intended to be a burden on them for the rest of her life, they
could have really enjoyed her company. An enormous thankful-
ness that she hadn't exploited them, hadn't brought them to the
brink of poverty, arose in them, mixed with admiration, yes,
even with sadness and loss. That Mrs. Arnold who cried and
ate fish balls in the woods and was nothing but a tiresome
hanger-on, appeared to be an unfortunate mistake, a kind of
optical illusion. Here stood the real one on the deck in traveling
dress, not in the least dependent; she had even given Andrine
a twenty-kroner tip. Andrine had sat, overcome, on the woodbox in the kitchen and dried her eyes with an apron corner at
departure time. You couldn't deny it. Mrs. Arnold had played
the winning card.

The bell rang for departure. Trembling a little, Mrs. Isaksen managed, "I hope we'll hear from you when you have the opportunity – a few lines, I mean – you understand, it will interest us how it goes with you..."

Mrs. Arnold wasn't made of stone either; she gave her a firm handshake and said, "That..."

But she pulled back her hand a little quickly perhaps, and her voice faltered as she continued, "you'll certainly get." For a moment it looked as if she wanted to say more, but nothing came of it. There was only good-bye and renewed expressions of thanks.

When the steamer sailed from the dock, the Isaksens waved, one and all, as if to a beloved family member off to America. And Mrs. Arnold waved back, walking along the railing and waving with the handkerchief until the steamer went around the point and she could neither see nor be seen any longer. Then she hurried into the smoking cabin after her things, placed them in the lee of one of the benches on the deck and sat down with them. Something windblown and tired and subdued came over her; her face and back collapsed a little. After an hour had gone by and the call for the first sitting for dinner had come, she took out a packet of biscuits from Flåten's and ate some of them. And when she was certain no one was looking she smuggled out bits of sausage for the biscuits from a piece of wrapped paper. Mrs. Arnold was traveling deck class and wasn't really going anywhere. She sat there, growing smaller and smaller in the blanket she'd tucked around her against the evening cold. The hours went by and she became a nodding dark silhouette against the white enameled wall behind her.

Toward dawn, when the sky had begun to lighten over the hills in the east, she got off, as if on impulse, at one of the landing places, went ashore and stood like a shadow in the gray light on the wharf, while the steamer departed and went on. She stood looking around and shivering; she took a few stumbling steps in the direction of a low rural building with HOTEL in large letters on it. The man on duty, yawning and in rubber boots, came down and took her bags....

*

On the way home the Isaksens were silent. Not until they swung into the yard did Mrs. Isaksen say, as if finishing a train of thought, "Well, anyway — we were probably of some help to her...."

But on the dining table lay an opened letter. Andrine had found it on the window sill. It was addressed to Mrs. E. Arnold, care of Mr. Isaksen, Merchant.

"There, you see — if only we had her address." Mrs. Isaksen turned and twisted the letter. "Well, I'll just have to take care of it in the meantime."

Inspired by the mood of the wharf and by the most honorable intentions, Mrs. Isaksen wandered into the bedroom, letter in hand, in the direction of the chest of drawers. This kind of thing should be locked up, not left to lie around. Naturally it wasn't her intention to read it. But there was no indiscretion in looking at the postmark.

It was from the nearest post office, a few kilometers away. Who in the world was Mrs. Arnold in correspondence with there? And whose handwriting was it? Mrs. Isaksen was suddenly certain she'd seen it before.

The letter came out of the envelope. Oh God, it wasn't really right, but...

Mrs. Isaksen's face grew blank in wonder. Grew blanker and blanker...

The letter was nothing more than a piece of white paper. There wasn't one word on it. And the writing on the envelope — that was certainly Mrs. Arnold's own! Mrs. Isaksen had stolen past her, peeking over her shoulder, all too often as she'd sat writing, to be in doubt of *that* any longer.

On one of her wanderings Mrs. Arnold sent herself a piece of white paper folded together in an envelope. The postmark was two days old.

Mrs. Isaksen sat down on her bed. She stared into space, stared at the letter, stared into space again, tried to understand.

"My mind is blank," she mumbled. "Is she crazy or am I?"

While a blush rose slowly on her face.

# *Thank You, Doctor*

"S sst, cat, don't stare!"

"Don't stare, you hear! Purr, cat!"

She says cat, she notices that herself. Never in her life has she said that before. She's said kitty. It makes her look directly at her own desperation.

With her hands in front of her face she peeks between her fingers at the cat. It keeps staring. The yellow eyes are like two lights in the jungle, lying in wait in the dark.

The cat has a tendency, when she's alone with it in the evening, to curl up into a ball under the bed, so that it's indistinguishable from the shadows. And to gaze.

As long as it purrs it's all right. But then it suddenly stops and just stares. And then she grows frightened. A long outgrown terror of the dark seizes her. The cat is no longer such a good-natured, playful, ordinary animal; it's mysterious and terrifying. As if paralyzed she sits there and stares back to defend herself.

For long periods she's not able to move a muscle. As if they were bound to each other, she and the cat.

It's as if the cat understands that. As if it wants that. Cats are extraordinary creatures.

With a start she pulls herself together, grips the lamp and holds it down to the floor. The cat grows visible against a background of flickering light. Her hand shakes.

"I see you all right. You're just a cat, nothing but a cat. Don't pretend otherwise. Why don't you purr?"

The cat lies there without moving. Its eyes contract to narrow slits against the brightness of the light. She sets the lamp back in place. At the same time she breaks out in a sweat. Fear and trembling. It's as real as it can be, not just something written down in the Bible.

Exhausted, she lays her head upon the table, turns it so her throat is fully illuminated and extended toward the cat. Let it come, let it jump at her. "Go ahead then, go ahead," she whispers.

They jump for the throat, she's heard. They see that something's alive in there, something's moving. Something to lie in wait for, to attack, play with, kill...

Then she remembers that cats see best in the dark and she laughs derisively at herself and her maneuverings. "You're such a fool."

She bends down and coaxes the cat. "Come on, Puss! Come and lie in my lap! Like during the day! We're *friends*, Puss, just good friends!"

She beseeches the cat, begs nicely. It doesn't move. Stares.

But when she's been sitting a while with slack hands and dull eyes, finished with her fear, only tired, it comes, hops in her lap, treading around a little while she makes a place for it. Then it curls up and purrs loudly.

Mechanically she pets it and cries quietly. She looks down at herself, sees her body bulge out where it should go in, above the cat. That uncooperative body that is only carrying out its function.

"We should go down and look after the heat, Puss. We don't dare do that, either. It's going out, it may already have gone out. We can't manage anymore, Puss. Not one thing. It's raining, Puss."

Behind the windowshade the autumn rain whips against the glass and runs down it. The stream from the rain gutter pours loudly on the ground. It's an evening when it should be nice to sit at home, dry and warm; a positive joy. The room has the coziness created by small means and a real sense of beauty. The colors are good, so are the reproductions on the wall; the lampshade is right. Through a draped doorway the lamp glow falls over an easel and other painting paraphernalia; it dies away in the darkness of a large room. Out there the rain drums on the skylights.

As if she were threatened by something from that side as well, she walks over with the cat on her arm and pulls the drapes together. On the way back to the chair she suddenly stops still with a faraway look, as if feeling for something deep inside, as if following an inner process with expectation and dread. She sits down immediately afterwards with an empty expression, stroking the cat as before. It purrs.

"Nothing, Puss. Nothing is happening. Nothing is going to happen. We're done for, Puss."

She hunches over the cat, presses her face down in its fur and wails, "I can't take it, I can't take anymore. They can take my life instead — put an end to me too at the same time...."

Her voice gets hoarse with fear; she cries hysterically.

The cat twists around, reaches out with its paws for her hair, thinks she wants to play.

From far away comes the sound of a streetcar. She hears it, lifts her head, dries her eyes, attempts to become herself again, all the while shaken by lengthy sobs.


A key is inserted in the outer door, the light switched on loudly and a pair of galoshes kicked off. A frank, unreserved masculine voice calls hello from out in the hall.

"Hello," she answers without moving.

"I'm here early, you see. As early as I could manage without being noticed."

Another light is switched on. Light from the outer room becomes visible under the drapes. The steps stop in front of something out there, are heard again, stop again.

"His work, of course," she mumbles bitterly to herself. "His work would come first, even if you were lying dead in here."

Then she pulls herself together, gets her face ready. "Try to be rational," she continues to mumble.

Steps again. He goes over to the radiator and touches it. "It's cold in here," he says. "It hasn't gone out, has it?"

"Don't know. Didn't dare go downstairs."

"But good Lord – and you've pulled the drapes? Why have you closed them?" He flings the drapes to one side and stands there, his face wet and fresh from outdoors, in his best clothes, far from ready to deal with a fire that's gone out.

"I'm a coward, I know that..."

"Coward? We're not talking nonsense again, are we? You were so cheery when I left." He's gathered both her hands in one of his; he strokes her on the head with the other hand and talks as if to a child.

She pulls away.

"Still nothing?"

"Nothing! Nothing! Nothing!"

She shouts loudly, her voice shaking.

"Now, now, don't you see... It must be done sometime!" His face seems to crumble for an instant, then he throws himself into what he can, for the moment, deal with. "I'd better hurry down and see about the heat," he says, taking off his jacket and disappearing out into the hall and down the cellar stairs.

Through the open doors she hears him down there, hears the rattling of the grate and the damper. The whole little house resounds when he pushes the poker up through the ash and cinder, twisting and turning, long and thoroughly.

She scrunches up at the sound as if she were the object being mistreated. As if she had to close her body up against a break-in. Then she whispers against her teeth, "No, don't get crazy, don't get crazy."

In the meantime he goes energetically about his task in the cellar. "Thank God there are still some live coals," he calls upstairs, keeping her posted. "They just need air – then I'll be able – to save them this time, too!" He maneuvers the poker with strength and expertise; when he takes a shovelful of coal it sounds like an avalanche under the floor. You can hear that the pile isn't large.

He's got it going down there. A little warmth has come into the pipes. Now they're sitting together. Have to talk to each other.

"Were there many people?" she asks, just to say something.

"The same as usual. Not a festive mood, though. I was glad to get out of there. Said I had to go home and write to *you*. There were a few questions about you, of course. You weren't coming for a few days yet, I said. Thought it was best to...."

He looks uncertainly at her. She doesn't answer.

"It was good I went anyway. I mean..."

"It certainly was."

The tone she uses isn't kind, but he takes it well. He looks over at the table that has nothing on it and asks patiently, "Well, what have you been doing?"

"Nothing. Sitting here."

"You're making it as unpleasant for youself as you can!"

"Am I?"

"But that's how women are. It's their nature,·I suppose."

"Maybe so."

The cat has jumped down from her lap and is rubbing against his leg. He takes it by the forepaws and lifts it up on two legs. "Um-hmm, Puss — that's how they are, you know — as dreary as possible — as difficult as possible — and as nasty and gloomy and hopeless as possible..."

"While you are all apostles of light and happiness."

"Huh!" He sighs and keeps talking to the cat. "Things are going to improve, Puss, for all of us. Otherwise it would be pretty bad." He gets up and tries to stroke her head again. She pulls away.

"Well, I'll go back in again tomorrow." Clearly it's no plea-sure excursion he's making. It's something he can't see any way around.

She hides her face in her hands. "I can't take anymore — I can't anymore — I won't anymore — I can't stand it — I'll go crazy...."

He comforts her as best he can. "There, there, don't take it like that. What in hell do you want us to do? The sooner the better – not to put it off any longer. I'll just have to go and say it hasn't helped, that... You have to understand that I think this is hell, too," he bursts out.

"Give me poison, give me something to kill myself with, ask him for that instead."

"Yes, of course..."

"Now you'll both start in on me again..."

"Would you think a minute about what you're saying..."

"He will then," she allows, unwillingly and without conviction.

He sighs again. But still takes it well, only mentions that she wanted it herself – she didn't see any other way, either. And now there's only one thing to do.

"Besides." He throws out his arms and then clamps them to his body again, bewildered, helpless. "I'll say it again, for the twentieth time, what would happen to us? To us – and you yourself? Your work? You were working so well. You said it too: I'll have to give up everything, you said. Those were your own words. For my part, I'd have to take up road construction – turn painting into a hobby! We'd have to leave the house. Finally we have a decent roof over our heads – a good studio, but... We'd have to go live in the woods.

"When I see what happens to others in our position. Pure misery for both them and the child. Yes, you know it yourself – when this is over you'll see how happy and relieved you'll be..."

"Happy. If I'd known the kind of maltreatment...," her voice breaks.

But here he has to correct her. "Actually," he says, "if we'd just been more resolute. We went along, waiting and hoping for..."

"It to be an illness..."

"It's totally impossible to talk to you when you're like this. But – it's going to be better, don't you think?" His tone is resigned, as if he's fully prepared that it won't be.

He begins to speak with the voice of reason, patient and well thought out: "*One* more time. He did say it might possibly be necessary. And then it's over. *Then it's over.* We're free again. *You* are free again. You can go out like before, think about your work like before; you won't need to go around hiding yourself from people any longer. Let's be a little sensible now. Here we meet a total stranger, who doesn't know any more about us than we tell him — well, he did know me as a painter, and you too, of course — and who's humane enough to — who won't take a penny — who, out of pure compassion...! He could have turned us *in*. Instead he comes out here, all the way from the city — one, two *three* times. You don't have to go to the Red Cross clinic or anything — well, I'll give him a sketch after a suitable amount of time has passed, and you should too, it's not too much. I'll go to town tomorrow, so we'll have an end to it."

He's shifted into a good-natured, encouraging tone, a very kind tone; he pats her on the head and back. And she gives in, cries against his shoulder, blows her nose, dries her eyes. When, later at some point, he says more or less the same thing again, earnestly and pleasantly, she nods mutely.

II

"I'm cold."

"Weren't you too warm a minute ago?"

"I'm cold."

"You think you might have a little fever?"

A little fever! In between attacks of pain and dozing, of heat and trembling cold, she has a few amazingly clear, quietly lucid moments when she hears, sees and perceives things more sharply than ever before in her life. During one of them she thinks, Tonight maybe I'll die.

She pauses a second at the thought. Die? Yes, it's strange,

of course it's strange. But it's as if it doesn't concern her. As if it really applies to another person.

He sits up reading. The sound of the pages he's turning in these moments becomes a hideous noise, an ear-deafening rustling. The hand that rests on her or that straightens the handkerchief he's hung over the lamp so the light doesn't bother, grows fearfully large. Instinctively she moves her head when it comes near.

In the glow of the lamplight pouring into the other room she can see her own easel with the still life on it. She also sees the low table with the sawed-off legs and some of the objects on it: a Dutch jug, some apples in a bowl, others lying here and there – the motif of patient and cheap things, the kinds of things everybody has, the resort of all penniless painters.

She knows a lot about those apples lying there shriveling up, about the jug and the bowl. Hour after hour she's studied them, brought out every æsthetic value, every reflection from somewhere else. And yet she's never really seen them before. They cast shadows, black, dark as night; they're hardly the light, innocent objects they pretend to be.

Him? Is he what he pretended to be? Now he's turning his head; his eyes meet hers. A concerned expression comes into them, encouraging, certainly loving. But not quick enough, not so quickly that she didn't see the calm expectation that was in them before. The calm of those who know that now all they have to do is wait patiently, that now things are going the way they're supposed to. Oh – he's not even a human being; he's a symbol, a symbol of eternal patience, able to wait and wait through anything, provided...

Provided...?

She looks away from him, looks at the ceiling, sends her thoughts in another direction: This man, this work, these two rooms, my household here, the patch of garden I've grown to love so much – perhaps I'll give my life for it. To keep it as it was. I cared for it so much that I lay down at the edge of the abyss to protect it. Too far out – I may tumble off at any moment and be lost in the darkness. Is that necessary? Isn't it just stupid?

Stupid, something deep inside says. But this doesn't concern her greatly, either. She feels she's powerless against it. It's simply too late to set it right.

She also thinks, They can't reach me; either I get through this or I get away. He'll have to answer all the questions about how it all came about. They're picky about that; the police could come. It won't be easy, I pity him. Perhaps he'll give the wrong answers. He's a symbol and doesn't even know it....

The pain grips her again, comes from deep inside and works its way out until it fills her body. A wave of heat gushes over her; everything is drowning in torture and terror. She's no longer aware of anything....

But at some point, when she opens her eyes, it's morning. Gray light fills the room like a thin fog in spite of the window-shade and the lighted lamp, forgotten and superfluous. Things are in the process of changing back to their old accustomed places. If she'd dozed a little longer everything would have been as usual: the lamp switched off, the shade up, all traces of the night obliterated. Now she's caught in the middle of its change.

She feels that it's over. She's not dead, won't die this time. A calmness has entered her body, a good, constant warmth. She brooded over horrible things throughout the night, unforgettable, frightening things. Now they've left her; it's as if she's numb. But she's not through with them. They'll come again. All bad dreams do.

He sits nodding, his head at an angle, snoring occasionally. He doesn't have a tie, his shirt is open, his hair disordered, sticking up in tufts. In the gray light he looks like he's been on a terrible bender. Sympathy for him creeps through her, but unwillingly and disapprovingly, the same kind one has for strangers who are their own worst enemies and lie by the side of the road. The wrong sort of feeling. She doesn't want to acknowledge it; she wants him to wake up so she can escape it. She starts to say something, to wake him, but it comes to nothing. She looks the other way.

Over. It's over. A needle of suspicion had jabbed at her, and then...

She finally brought herself to mention it one day. She'd been fighting with it a long time by then, one moment fearful, the next unbelieving.

He was beside himself. They couldn't afford it. She knew that just as well as he did – knew that it was a question of life and death, so to speak, their work and everything... she could only agree. All the same – wasn't it then that her coldness began. *Then* that she began to grow wicked? What was it she really wished for, in her innermost heart? Something completely insane?

The conversations in bed at night. You could get help, you just had to look for it. This wasn't the Middle Ages anymore – this was an enlightened era. He'd heard of several who went around openly.

Fear of it, of how it would be, of the risk if they were discovered, of being sick afterwards...

But he could reassure her on that point. Some people went to quacks, fell into ignorant hands. That mustn't happen in this case of course.

Her reluctance to entrust herself to a stranger.

Finally she set off one day. Her heart banged in a strange spot, up on one side of her throat, and wouldn't stop. Everyone in the waiting room looked like they knew all about it and the doctor gave the impression of seeing right through her from the beginning. Over his desk hung a plaster mask of Beethoven. That also made it difficult. She couldn't take her eyes off it. Even at the moment the examination was over, when a voice said, yes, it was true, and the knowledge sank in her like a stone to the bottom and remained lying there – it was the plaster mask she saw.

She couldn't manage to get a word out about what she'd come for. She was on her way to the door when the conversation began...

Yes, they were both artists – yes, these were difficult times, no one was buying anything.... No, no home to fall back on,

no relatives at all. She would have to stop painting, look for
something else, put the child out to be nursed. Yes — they were
in debt, too, rather a lot. The situation was desperate; they
hadn't intended to start a family so soon. How old she was?
Twenty-five and a half. Yes — she was the one who had the
paintings at the State Exhibit in the fall. Yes, she had to be
satisfied with the reviews. No, no sales unfortunately. Oh no,
the house wasn't theirs...they rented it. Yes, it was on the
Bærum streetcar line.

She heard herself answering as if to questions in a lesson.
It was important to answer correctly — this answer to that question, to answer truthfully, the way it was. The lesson was easy
as far as that went, if you could only keep your mind on it.

When she left she had his brief assurance that she would
get help, even if she were very far gone. A new disquiet gnawed
at her. What would happen now?

Shame. That's what she felt. Shame and disgrace and torment. It made her wicked, wrong-headed and mean. Everything seemed bewitched; she no longer saw light in front of her,
she felt as if she'd been driven into a trap that was making her
crazy.

She's escaped it now. The future lies ahead as it did before.
Something stood in her way, looming, threatening. It's been
rolled away, blasted off. Work, possibilities, everything she
and he had together, poverty and difficulties notwithstanding
— everything she was afraid of losing — it lies ahead, lies ahead.

She didn't scream during the night, she knows that. Not
even during the worst moments. Now she cries. Quietly, without a sound, but also without end. Tears flow and flow as if
from an underground spring. Not just of tiredness. She should
be happy now. But it's not just out of tiredness she cries.

His book falls to the floor. He starts up, sees her.

"Well? I dozed off, didn't I?"

"It's over."

"Is it over?"

He gets up abruptly. "But then, good Lord, I mean — you
shouldn't be crying, should you? After all, it's — over — then..."

He strokes her cheek, awkward, well-meaning; he's not sure at first what he should do. He smooths his hair, pets the cat who's also awake and rubbing against his leg. "It's over, Puss, over..."

"Are you sure?" he asks, suddenly gripped by mistrust.

"Yes, of course I am. You'll have to go get him."

"Yes, of course." He looks at the clock, switches off the lamp, rolls up the windowshade. Outside it's broad daylight – a clear, beautiful autumn morning. "It's going to be a fine day," he says. "We're going to have good weather from now on, you'll see. Soon you'll be outside again, you can sit in the garden..."

"Where did you tell the others I went?"

"To – Hønefoss – to an aunt's. Why do you ask?"

"I can't have been so exhausted by a trip to Hønefoss that I have to sit in the garden, can I?"

"I only meant..."

"We have to think about these things now."

"Of course we have to."

"Maybe I should sit with a blanket wrapped around my legs and a pillow at my back."

The calm coolness of her voice makes her completely unapproachable. And these tears that keep rolling down her face. She doesn't move, doesn't look up.

"But aren't you happy?" he blurts out, helpless.

"Of course."

He doesn't know what else to try. He talks about coffee, about a really good cup of coffee – he'll go make it. About the taxi he's going to take, so the doctor can get here right away.

She cries.

He leaves then. This is probably the reaction they talk about, nerves and so on. It's no wonder; it probably takes time. So he leaves.

She opens her eyes and gets a glimpse of how he stretches himself outside the door. Just a little, just for a second. As after a good walk, a well-performed mission. And before an approaching rest.

The little house wakes up. From the cellar comes the

avalanche sound of coal, from the kitchen the smell of coffee; the cat purrs loudly. Today it will get its dish of cream earlier than usual. Life is all around her, the life she was afraid of having destroyed for her.

He brings the coffee on a nicely arranged tray; he's cleaned himself up, looks newly washed and combed, not a bit sleepy or tired any longer. He will take the streetcar in – that's always a small savings. He'll catch the first one, on that one he won't meet anyone they know. If it had happened during the night he would have had to take a taxi both ways. Just think, it's really over – this terrible time is over – to be perfectly honest, he was more than a little worried.

He holds out the cup and she drinks eagerly. But otherwise she is as unapproachable as before, silent and in tears. So he contents himself with saying that she should just lie there quietly and rest now. In a half hour at the most they'll be back. *At the most.*

She hears the hall door, the outer door, his steps on the gravel outside. A brisk, healthy man's quick, firm steps. Now he's running. The latch clicks back on the garden gate. There's the streetcar.

And she waits. While everything that happened during the night comes back to her, takes shape.

Money, money, money.

Those who don't have it don't even own their own bodies. But those who have it shake their heads mournfully, full of bittersweet wisdom. "Money's not everything, far from it."

That's their position. It's shrewd enough, fitting enough. But the rest of us have to pay for the most ordinary things with all we own – work, future, our lives. Or let ourselves be mutilated.

Money's not everything. But it's the key to the rest. That's how it is. Now she knows. That's how they've arranged the world. Who? *Them.*

Strange thoughts rage through her. Since last night everything has turned upside down, inside out, wrongside out. Or rightside? God knows. Was she blind before? Or is she now?

These two men on their way? She was in love with one of them. She wanted to continue feeling that, told herself over and over that there was no other way, she couldn't ask the impossible from him. Toward the other man she was grateful, told herself that he was kind and helpful and that's how life was, she just had to accept it. She's no longer in love, isn't thankful. They've turned into a single enemy for her. Her soul is hard and dead.

Two men! Why hadn't she understood before what two men mean? Loyalty far surpassing what any woman could comprehend. She believed they were on *her* side. No, they were against her. That's how she sees it now; she's unable to see it any other way. A burden, they're afraid to have a burden; they understand that about each other.

And what about her? She who went along with it. Let it happen to her. Is she any better? No, she's worse. Both body and soul spoke up in time, refused and flinched. But there were two of them, and one of her, and she alone had to suffer, completely alone. That's how they arranged it. Who? *Them*.

She looks around, looks at things from the night. They stand there, almost as if they want to make her believe that everything is as before. It's no use. They're withered, they're dead, irrelevant. No magic light surrounds them any longer.

Her thoughts wander confusedly.

She dozes off. Wakes again at the sound of keys and footsteps, doors opening, men's voices.

It's taken from her. Something is carried away in a bucket.

She gets up then and looks. For her own good they try to prevent her. They're not able to.

Something murdered, something tiny and bloody, small limbs...

She doesn't say anything, just lies down again. But they come over at once. She mustn't take it like that. Why did she want to? There was no reason for her to....

She doesn't answer. For there are no words. A feeling shoots up from deep inside, cuts through her like lightning. A desperate need to give shelter and warmth, to cherish and protect: tenderness and rage. Something had sought shelter inside her, something completely helpless. There they go with it....

It can't be talked about.

She closes her eyes, lies there hearing them say encouraging things. She's been a trooper and now it's all over. Calmer days are coming again, work, the old routine. Soon she'll be up and hard at work. The spring exhibition is coming in a few months...

She thinks — they're lying. It will never be over. It's irremediable. More is dead than they suspect. I'll never be a really nice person again, not in the old way. I'll have to pretend. As long as it's to my advantage...

She opens her eyes a moment and says very correctly, "Thank you, doctor."

# The Child

YOU MIGHT THINK you were in a corner of paradise. But if anything, this place is its complete opposite. Who would have thought it looked like this?

A Raggedy Andy sits on the sofa. With clear black pearl eyes he stares off into the distance.

Potted plants in full bloom stand on the window sill – fuschias, geraniums. The curtains are of a light, airy material. They flutter in the summer breeze outside. A couple of windows are open. Their panes are shiny and clear.

There are books on the table. Shelves around hold more. Many books, a little of everything. About life and death and love, in verse and in prose. A piece of needlework is out, a little dainty nothing of thin lace and thin silk, a garment soft as baby skin.

The piano is open. Choice music, old and new, is propped up on the noteholder. Chopin. Scriabin.

Sometimes a child comes through the door, goes across the room, takes Raggedy Andy on his lap and chats with him, searches through the books on the table for one with pictures in it, plunks with one finger on the piano. A wholesome child, with bare arms and legs, brown from sun and wind, dirty in the clean way children tend to get – from rolling around in the sand and grass, wading on the beach, baking mudpies, braiding long stalks of dandelions, eating chocolate.

He has a happy child's open, carefree gaze; he has no idea where he is.

*

But grown-ups frequent this place too, a woman, a man. They know where they are.

The woman comes and goes. She waters the flowers, straightens up, dusts the furniture, sits down occasionally with a book or with the needlework that is out, takes a few stitches, never many. There are pieces of needlework that get nowhere; this is one of them. There are also books that will never be read, just leafed through. They lie there and can't make themselves heard; time after time they're slammed shut and shoved aside.

She is restless. Scarcely has she sat down than she's up again, giving herself something new to do, over here, over there – rubbing a window pane that was completely clear already, going over a polished surface one more time with the duster, undertaking many unnecessary things. For a moment she hums. But she also brushes away a tear or two that suddenly appears at the corner of her eye and that threatens to slip down her cheek. She is slender and dark.

Sometimes she comes in, with wet hands and a hungry expression on her face. Angrily she dries her hands on her apron and throws herself at the piano. And a drama breaks loose. Two voices chase each other. The one taunts, the other follows and persecutes it, begging, threatening. They catch each other, unite savagely, in pain and happiness.

Suddenly the whole thing breaks into grinding dissonance. She bangs both hands on the piano keys so the instrument protests loudly. She falls forward with her head on the keys and it protests again. Tears drip through her fingers.

But she can also play a nocturne as softly as if it were really nighttime and she were playing someone to sleep. And her cheeks only become a little damp.

Sometimes she gets up and dances a waltz in the middle of the room.

Sometimes she starts walking from wall to wall with long, soundless steps like an animal in a cage. It always ends with her taking out her handkerchief.

She hears the child coming and rubs her face energetically, changing her expression as routinely as an actor. The child runs in, leaving the door open after him, throwing himself into his mother's lap in tears or laughter like all small children. Or he has flowers and hands her a bouquet, made up of all kinds of weeds, one short stalk, one long, something completely impossible to put in a vase, but which she puts in water anyway. There it is, Heavens, how pretty!

Occasionally the child falls and scrapes himself, displaying a dirt-gray little fist, a round knee, with gravel ground in and a trace of blood. He whimpers, he calls for his mother, must be helped and comforted. No one is easier to comfort. Soon the child is laughing again, sitting on the sofa with his Raggedy Andy in his arms and a bandage on his scrape, sucking on something sweet and looking at a picture book. His mother laughs and chats with him, keeping him occupied, over and over again taking him on her lap to kiss him. There's a touch of self-reproach in her manner, a touch of anxiety. She sings little snatches, tells short fairy tales, "Once upon a time there was a tiny, tiny, tiny little woman who lived in a tiny, tiny, tiny little house..."

The child listens with shining eyes, full of expectation. But suddenly the mother loses the thread and can't find it again. Absent-minded and troubled, she pushes the child down from her lap. "All right, go out and play a little now. We can't sit inside the whole day."

The child goes. Without acting surprised. This is the kind of thing that happens. It has happened many times.

Toward evening the mother hears the gate swing open, hears the sound of a man's step on the gravel path. The restlessness in her face changes to something closed and tense.

She goes quickly around the room, closing the piano, putting away the music, sweeping away her own traces. For a moment she stands, needlework in hand, undecided, then she leaves it lying on the table.

And she leaves the room.

The man comes in.

He is what is called a handsome man, correct, confidence-inspiring, well groomed, in his best years. Without a doubt a pleasant man as well, who should have the right to count on peace and quiet when he comes home. He doesn't count on it. Watchfully and suspiciously he looks around, biting his lip, muttering to himself.

The child has come in with him. He stands leaning against his father's knee, full of things he wants to share. He's seen a squirrel, a sweet little squirrel. He's seen the hedgehog, that sweet little hedgehog. He's picked a pretty bouquet for mother. There it is.

"Yes, pretty!"

The father takes the child in his lap. But his thoughts are elsewhere.

The child wants to be entertained. He brings out the picture book, sits and points to things in it. The father says mechanically, "Yes, such a sweet pussycat. Yes, such a nice hen."

He watches the door, he listens. Suddenly he shoves the child off his lap, dashes to the telephone, hastily dials a number and is in the midst of a conversation when the mother enters.

He neither sees nor hears her; he talks and laughs in high spirits, a man occupied with his own private friends and pleasures. Not even after he's hung up does he think of her; he continues to sit paging through the directory for more numbers, more distracting connections to friends.

"Hello," she says lightly and sits down.

"Oh, you're here? Hello."

"Well?"

There is impatience in her voice, but also childlike expectation. She's disappointed. He shrugs his shoulders. "Yes – no – nothing special."

She sits there. As if she has waited in vain for something unusual. And she has. She's continually waiting for this man to say something he doesn't say; she's waited every minute of their life together. What, she's not sure of, only that he doesn't say it now, either.

"No," he gestures with two empty hands.

His day has been like all his other days. Nothing has happened. He's coming from the same monotony as yesterday and the day before, and he isn't an imaginative man for whom even the gray everyday is full of adventure. He's not an emotional man, either, with feelings that ebb and flow and break out unexpectedly. He instinctively acts, as best he can, the enigma you can't pin down – calling to imaginary friends on the telephone and so forth. But that role doesn't suit him well; he can't pull it off and it's against his nature to try. His personality is open and calm.

It doesn't help matters either. She sits there as rebellious and unreasonable as before. Her disappointment, her completely unjust disappointment still hangs uncomfortably in the air, making him become even more buttoned up than he really is. What the devil does she want?

"Well – and what about you?" His mouth curls ironically.

"Fine, thanks," she answers, just as ironically.

He strikes out at the feeling of discomfort and falls right into a trap. He takes the needlework and clumsily holds it up. "Only a woman could have the time and patience for this sort of thing, that's for sure."

"Time! Oh, good Lord, that's been lying around for weeks. If I only had the time to..."

She has him there. Plagued, he looks around, looks at the piano. It's closed. No music is out. He's been stopped cold by the great myth, the immense, engrossing, all-devouring myth known as managing a house, which demands sacrifice beyond comprehension. He's paralyzed by it for a moment.

But he comes to himself again and seizes on the needlework as useful pretext for a new attack. "I don't believe I've seen this before."

"There are one or two things you don't see," she says and gets up. "Come along, it's time to eat."

At the same time she laughs loudly and scornfully, too loudly.

"Think a little about..." Reproachfully he inclines his head in the direction of the child, who looks up wonderingly.

"I don't think of anything else. If I did..."

"If you did...? He stares at her provokingly.
"Oh!"
Taking the child by the hand, she leaves the room. "Come, let's you and I go wash ourselves up a little."


Amazingly, the food is like ordinary, well-prepared, down-to-earth, everyday food. Fried mackerel, new potatoes, a pint of beer, pudding. It ought to taste good.

And it does taste good to him, at least to begin with. He thinks he's encouraging the ceasefire. "This is good," he says tentatively.

"Is that so," she answers coldly. "That's nice then."

After that they both talk with the child. Mechanically they both say the kinds of things that adults inevitably, always say to children.

"So what have you been doing today?"

"Use your right hand, my boy."

"Have you been with the other children?"

"No, no, now you've made a mess of mother's clean table-cloth. You mustn't hold your spoon that way. You must hold it like *this*."

"And the chickens next door? How are they doing?"

"Don't just eat potatoes. Eat your fish too. That's it."

The child answers right and left, in the belief that he is the most important person at the table; he doesn't see that the ground is shaky, that this is just where life lays its dangerous traps.

The cat has caught a chick. And the mother hen has trampled on another, she doesn't know any better, poor thing. It broke its leg, so they had to kill it, kill that sweet little chick. But now it's buried and it has a cross and a peony on its grave. And fish isn't good when you're full.

The child twists and turns in his chair, doesn't want to eat his fish. The parents continue fencing through the child.

"You don't have to then."

"Eat it up now, please."

"Maybe we gave you too much. Maybe there's not enough room in that little stomach of yours."

"Now then, let's not fuss. Be a good boy and finish up or else there won't be any pudding."

The child declares he's pudding-hungry, not fish-hungry. He leans back in his chair and sits beating the plate with his spoon. He's not sitting nicely at the table and his mother wants to send him away. Without pudding.

But his father sets the pudding in front of him, fetching it himself from the sideboard and sprinkling sugar on it. "Now let's not discuss it anymore. There's a limit to the demands we can make in the summer heat. We should be a little flexible under the circumstances."

So, now he's assuming the role of master of the house for once. He's also managed to get in a double meaning. Very good.

The child starts in on his pudding. But he looks from one to the other, uneasy, shy. The first unclear feeling that life is less than secure shoots through him just then.

His parents don't exchange another word.


Evening has arrived. A summer evening with heavy, quiet, dark masses of leaves against a sky as fragile and light as glass, but which grows darker after a while, so that a few stars slip through. The smell of hay, clover and roses. An untiring cricket somewhere in the grass. A landscape more like paradise than ever.

In the room with the piano the hanging lamp is lit. Night moths buzz against the closed windows. Some windows are open and moths whirl in, to be caught in the hanging lamp; they don't come out again, they continue to buzz and buzz against the opaque glass. You can see them behind it like dumb, helpless little shadows.

*He* sits in here.

He's put down his newspaper and sits staring at the moths. It's no use trying to help them. You can only leave them alone until death takes pity on them. But he understands what it's like for them. He himself buzzed into a light once, and it's damned different being inside than it appears outside. You think you've found a cozy embrace, a breast to rest against, bliss, peace. You get an opponent instead: capricious, incomprehensible, untiring. Music? Not a note. The piano stands there dumbly, a symbol of injury, an accusation against him. If he didn't long so terribly to be close to her, only her, the child's mother, he'd want to get away, far away.

From the garden he hears her steps. *She* is wandering around out there.

She walks and walks; the gravel crunches underfoot. Sometimes she stops and then the stillness is so heavy with suppressed things he can't identify that he moves uneasily in his chair.

She sees the moths too; she too thinks about them flying into the light. She herself flew into something believing it would be an eternally new experience, blissful madness without end. She's walking here, consumed by longing for new, continually new expressions of exactly the same eternal things – longing for him, the child's father. She's torn to pieces by yearning for the strange man whom she believes is sitting inside reading his newspaper, completely unaffected. And by bitterness against his constant self-composure.

But the child sleeps in a little white crib. He's kicked off his covers in the warmth and lies there with bare, brown, plump limbs and a face like a flower. The child is dreaming deeply; he's forgotten the stab of new and unexplained pain that ran through him only a short while ago. He doesn't suspect that he constitutes the living chain of flesh and blood and nerves binding two incompatible people together, and that he will have to pay for it. All in the course of time.

# The Flight to America

"FATHER! Where are you going, Father?"

Oddemann gets up from the grass in Leif's yard, stands there with his stomach out, his legs far apart, bareheaded, hair the color of gold straw, six years old this autumn, face dark as earth, with his overall knees stained green and both fists full of grass. Above and around him apple trees swell in blossom. In the flower bed's violet mold, carmine tulip petals on supple stalks gape open greedily to the sun. The air shimmers, light and warm. It's June. It's Sunday.

Leif's father is pushing the lawnmower, followed by Leif at his heels. The grass is short and dense like the gold rug at home in the parlor, good to turn somersaults on, to roll around on like a puppy. The big wheelbarrow is out.

But over on the road Odd sees his own father run down to the station on the wrong day and at the wrong time of day and with a small suitcase. The garden gate closes after him with a bang.

Odd and Leif were each supposed to get a lollypop when the grass was gathered and wheelbarrowed into a corner back by the lilac bushes, but suddenly Odd loses all interest. He dashes as fast as he can out to the road and after his father. He calls out to him. His father stops. It looks as if he'll come back again. But then he just waves and runs on. And Odd has to give up the chase.

He has a feeling he should go home now. Odd gets feelings like that. An unrest, a sudden longing surging up. His throat gets thick and strange then; he's not far from tears. But big boys don't cry. The only thing he can do is go.

"Are you leaving now, Oddemann?" calls Leif's father from Leif's yard. "I thought you were going to help us."

"Odd," calls Leif.

Oddemann just keeps on going.

He runs so that the dust flies. He smells like earth and grass, and fresh healthy youth that's been outside for hours; he smells of life. With one tight fist he rubs the corners of his eyes again and again and his face gets even blacker. At the gate he has to struggle with the lock, which is stuck. He runs up the path. He practically falls into the kitchen. "Katrine!" he calls. "Where is Father going?"

But Katrine isn't in the kitchen. No one is.

Odd hears his mother's voice from the hall and goes there. Mother is talking fast and loud, without pausing. Mother talks like that when she's being nasty. Odd opens the door anyway. He has a feeling he should. But carefully.

Mother is standing by the telephone, laughing loudly, even though she's angry, in the midst of saying, "...just like that, walked out, ha-ha-ha, as if you could just do that, just leave...Now, just a minute ago! What do you think of that? But he'll see what he's let himself in for, he'll come back and there'll be no one around, not a soul, ha-ha-ha, that'll be a lesson to him and maybe get him back to his senses...What are you saying? Bitter? Far from it, not one bit...Easy, take it easy. God, if there's anything I am, it's calm...Lawyer? Talk to a lawyer? We don't need a lawyer here, what we need is an undertaker, ha-ha-ha, just an undertaker. Well, come over if you think you have to, but I'm really completely calm. Katrine has the day off, but I can give you a cup of tea...."

Katrine is standing in the middle of the room. She has both hands over her ears and is moaning, "Lord Jesus, Lord Jesus! Off? No, I don't want the day off." She catches sight of Odd and goes over to Mother. "Oddemann, Ma'am."

Mother puts the receiver down. When Odd gets a look at her face he becomes horribly afraid. Is this Mother? She's no longer pretty; she is ugly, hideous with tears, even though she was standing there laughing; her upper lip is drawn up over her teeth and her hair is in disarray. She starts to laugh loudly again. "Ha-ha-ha, do you know what your father is? Do you know? Answer, boy!" She takes Odd by the shoulders and shakes him.

"Ma'am, ma'am," cries Katrine. Just then one of his mother's friends, one of the many he calls aunt, comes rushing through the kitchen door. Immediately afterwards he finds himself standing in the middle of the kitchen, led there in haste by Katrine. All he could hear was that Mother burst out sobbing when the parlor door shut on her and the aunt.

Totally bewildered he stands there. Isn't he supposed to know what his father is? What kind of question is that? He is the engineer H. O. Kvam, Villa Breidablikk, Nordstrandshøyden. Odd could have given the answer to that question if he hadn't been so scared. But he didn't get a chance, either. If he had, maybe Mother wouldn't have been so mad at Father. Odd sees that connection at least – that it's really Father she's mad at.

Katrine sits on a chair, dabbing her eyes with an apron corner.

Before he can stop himself Odd starts howling too, big boy that he is. He lays his head on the kitchen bench and roars. Out of continuing fear and because he didn't get to answer the question, because Katrine is crying and Mother is crying and Father is gone and something has fallen apart and there's talk of funerals.

"Don't cry, Oddemann."

"Where's Father going?"

"He's going to town, I suppose."

"But it's Sunday," shouts Odd and sobs. "He wouldn't go to town on Sunday. Not without Mother."

"Mother's not well, Oddemann. We're going to call the doctor."

"Is Mother the one who's going to be buried?"

"Are you crazy, boy? Don't talk like that. No one is going to be buried, I should hope."

"But Mother said…"

"She didn't mean that, Oddemann, she didn't mean that."

"When is Father coming back?"

"Father…I don't know exactly," says Katrine uncertainly. "I don't think he'll be gone long," she adds, trying to be cheerful.

Odd finishes as suddenly as he began, both with tears and questions. They're always trying to fool you, make up something. Mother sick? He knows when his Mother is angry, even if she does laugh. They're not telling him where Father has gone, either. Odd stands looking out the kitchen window, a hand propping up his white-streaked dirty face.

Puss walks through the yard, comes up the steps with small, neat hops and slips through the door that is standing ajar. There she is, purring loudly, against Odd's leg.

Overwhelmed by a violent tenderness Odd bends down and collects the cat in his arms. She overflows his embrace, soft and warm and purring so it rumbles.

"Puss…Puss, Puss…you're so nice, Puss…."

Quietly Odd backs his way into his bedroom. He leaves the door open after him….

"What do you make of it, Sister?"*

It's one of the aunts talking, one of the ones who've run in and out the whole afternoon, telephoning, bringing the doctor, bringing the strange woman in a blue dress, white apron, and little stiff cap like an overturned bucket that she never takes off at the top of her tightly pulled-back hair.

"We see so much in our line of work, you know," answers the woman with the bucket.

"Of course you do, don't you? Many sad things."

Odd listens to them through the open door. While he is, to all appearances, eagerly occupied, building a house around Puss, a house constructed from the footstool, all the building

---

*In Scandinavia sister also means nurse. – Trans.

blocks and the day's paper. Puss lies there purring calmly, no matter what. She's an old and wise cat who knows her people, appreciates Odd's true value and honors him above all others with her confidence.

One thing is certain: that if Odd wants to understand what's really going on, he has to pretend he's totally occupied with other things. Then they believe you can't see or hear. Asking doesn't do any good, he knows from bitter, almost six-year-old experience. He's a master at drawing attention away from himself while watching and listening.

Someone says "shhh" out there; they whisper and sigh. Now they're discussing him. He catches "poor boy, someone should really..." But what someone should escapes him. On the other hand he hears "...not an easy boy...have tried to shoo him out the whole afternoon, but no..."

Suddenly the aunt is in his room, wanting to kiss him, saying, "Oh, look, such a darling house you're building, Odd. And if it isn't Puss sitting inside. No, you're so clever. It's really well done."

"Where did Father go?" says Odd, squirming under the kiss.

"He went to town, I suppose. He often goes to town, you know. Good-night, Oddemann."

"He never goes to town on Sunday," says Odd shortly. "Good-night."

The aunt sighs. The aunt leaves. He hears the front door close after her.

No, they'll see he's not an easy boy. An easy boy doesn't find out anything. He is a difficult boy.

The sun has gone down. The room is full of that slow summer twilight that makes small children anxious and sorrowful. That doesn't bring out night lights, new possibilities of any sort. That only brings an oppressive dusk that commands you to sleep when you're not sleepy.


"Little Odd should go to bed now." It's the one with the

bucket talking. She also says, "Come, let Sister help you."

Sister. She's not his sister, he won't let her be. Sisters are different; they're a little bigger or smaller than you, occasionally appearing unexpectedly, tiny like Lilletullen at Leif's house, but never turning up so suddenly and fully grown up as this one.

He told her that straight out when she arrived, when she was also going on about this "sister" business. She smiled and answered that she was everyone's sister, and that he would understand it better when he was big. That was the grown-ups' excuse when they didn't have an answer or wanted to pull the wool over your eyes.

"Come now, little Odd."

"You should be with Mother," says Odd and continues, "Katrine tucks me in when Mother can't."

"Katrine went to the pharmacy, dear. Mother is going to have a sleeping pill, so she can sleep. A nice aunt is sitting with Mother now."

Odd stops work on his construction, puts the blocks in the box, sets the footstool back in place and puts the newspaper back where he took it from, on the hall table. Puss comes into view, nicely settled, with her tail curled tightly around her body. She stops purring, creeps under a chair, closes pained eyes and agrees with him. Puss doesn't like Sister, either.

Odd puts himself at her disposal, standing there with his arms flat against his body and the inscrutable expression of children when they've given up all opposition and have submitted to odious circumstances.

To go to bed is, under any conditions, one of life's misfortunes. Today it's horrible. When this so-called sister has pulled down the venetian blind and gone her way, Odd will be lonely as never before in his life. They've taken Mother's bed out of the bedroom next door to his and put it somewhere in the apartment, perhaps in the parlor. Father hasn't come; the house around Odd is full of alarming secrets.

If only he could have Puss with him in bed! Puss herself is more than willing. Each evening she hides herself very understandingly and instinctively under the dresser until all intruders are gone. When it's been quiet a while, she hops up to Odd, to curl up together with him, nice and soft on the pillow, to purr loudly and cozily. But that sort of thing is forbidden. After a while Mother usually comes tiptoeing in to lift Puss out of the bed and to take her away. "I won't hear of that cat on the bed," she says. "Ugh." Sister has a small chance here.

Odd stands before her wearing only his shirt and knit underwear, buttoned up the back. He's had his face washed, then his neck and hands; he has to sit on a chair while she does his feet. Gone for the time being are Mother's vigorous splashes over his whole naked body every evening, her impatient, "Now we'll have to hurry up a little," with each piece of clothing supposed to go on or off. In spite of everything, some things have improved.

He says nothing, except to remind Sister not to forget his ears. It'll do her good to be corrected, even if it is at the cost of comfort. For Odd she is an integral part of the evil that has broken loose. Like Mother's anger and Father's absence and his own loneliness and fear.

But while she's wrapping the comforter around him — completely the wrong way, so that he'll have to get up in the creepy twilight to do it for himself when she's gone — he asks nonetheless, "Is Father coming back tonight?"

"I...I don't really know...maybe not tonight, but...he'll come back soon. Just sleep now, Odd...I'll leave the door open a little."

Without another word Odd lies down. And Mother or Katrine has said something, because Sister looks under the dresser to see if Puss has hidden there. Which Puss has. Sister has to squat to get at her. She carries the cat hanging over her arm, so tail and paws dangle painfully in the air, out with her. The way grown-ups carry cats. Odd hears her open the door to the kitchen, where, with an impatient, slightly exhausted, "So, out you go," she lets Puss fall any old way on the floor. There goes Sister's chance.

And night is there, painful to breathe.

Through the twilight Odd glimpses things around him. They close up around him and are different than in the day. Look at the dresser, how strange it is, thick-bellied and not very kind. And the stove! The stove is the worst, Odd knows that from other wakeful nights. He tries to force himself not to look at it. But whenever his eyes open a crack, there it is, gleaming black and ugly.

Once in a while he hears Mother. She is still talking loudly, angrily and without pausing. Distant doors are opened and closed, cutting her flow of speech into small pieces. It sounds as if she were crying out the same things over and over. Other voices also want to say something, but Mother shrieks still louder and drowns them out.

Suddenly a thought strikes Odd. It's so overwhelming that he has to sit straight up in bed. Father had a suitcase. Father's gone to America. Gone anyway, though Mother didn't want him to. They talked loudly yesterday evening in the bed-room and couldn't agree. Father didn't sleep in his bed last night but on the sofa in the hall. Odd had to get up early for something and he saw Father lying there then. Father looked up and said, "Is that you up and about, Oddemann?" By then Father had been absent for a little while already.

In America they steal children, shoot each other and have earthquakes so the houses fall down. He has heard Katrine talk about it with the washerwoman. The uncles and aunts say about America, "God, don't take such a chance, you don't know what you're doing; they say it's horrible there." Mother says, "No power on earth would make me go away in these times, to be without a maid and everything; no, thank you."

But Father always says, "The way things are at home now, I'd gladly leave tomorrow."

Odd lies down again but he shivers throughout his whole body. Until Father comes home again, nothing will go right. Not until then will Mother be gentle and the way Odd always wants her to be. The way she is when she sometimes kisses him good-night, kisses him a lot all over his face. Nothing is like

Mother's kiss, Mother's caress. When she puts her arms around his neck and lifts him a little as she turns the pillow, it's like being in a delicious nest, soft and lingering and sweet smelling. Every evening Odd longs for Mother to do that.

But when she boxes his ears, her hand is hard. Like a flat stone whistling in the air.

What is it?

Odd may have been asleep, but now he's wide awake. And there it is again, the buzzing noise of the telephone dial as it goes forward and then falls back with a small click. At the same time someone is talking out in the hall, thinly and monotonously and continually. It's like an endless sad little song. It takes a minute before Odd understands that it's Mother, it's Mother telephoning.

He listens, wondering. It's still night in the room, but from the hall a pale gray glow falls through the partially open door. Out there it's neither night nor day, but something in between, strange and sad. Mother is no longer angry, not one bit angry. Mother is sad and very tired.

Odd gets sad too, listening to her. He wishes he could do something. He wants to go out and put his arms around her neck. Yes...he wants to put his arms around her neck....

He remains standing in the open door. In the gray half light Mother sits with her head leaning against the wall and the receiver at her ear. With the other hand she turns the dial, uninterruptedly sticking a finger first in one hole, then in another, sometimes having many fingers in many holes at the same time. It looks like she's sitting and playing. She lets her fingers follow the dial back again, so that it makes more noise. She is in pajamas with her bare feet in slippers and it's almost like she's sleeping. Her eyes keep closing, then suddenly popping open again. She doesn't see Odd.

"...I loved you *too* much, you see...that was what I did... loved you *too* much...we get unreasonable then...and now you've left, even though it's June...June when people are in

love...and so lonely if they're alone...but I can't stand it, you
see, I can't manage it...and now I'm going to sleep and won't
feel anything any longer...my darling, my darling...."

Odd suddenly thinks how small Mother is. Mother is like
the little baby at Leif's house. She also babbles while she gets
sleepier and sleepier. They tuck her in carefully and sing her
lullabies and tiptoe out when she's fallen asleep. Someone
should do that for Mother, Odd sees clearly. She's talking to
Father in America, she is nice and gentle, and says my darling,
so Father has certainly promised to come back again. As soon
as Mother asks him to hurry a little, Odd wants to find something to cover her with and a pillow for her head and kiss and
lull her so she'll fall asleep.

He goes over and takes his mother's face in both hands.
"You're so small, Mother, so very tiny, but now Oddemann's
going to help you...."

Mother opens her eyes slightly. The receiver falls down into
her lap, lies there buzzing and whistling to itself. Mother throws
her arms around Odd, but slackly, so he understands that she
is very tired. With a faraway voice she says, "My boy, my boy."

And Odd is in the delicious nest again. He stands there,
barefoot on the floor, but with his head and arms in Mother's
lap. He is quiet and blissful and he whispers, "Talk more with
Father, Mother...talk more with him. Say he should come
home quick, say..."

And Mother hums softly once more. Like the little baby
at Leif's house.


You never know what's going on with grown-ups.

Odd is suddenly grabbed by one arm and slung aside. At
the same time it's like the doors burst open and shut of their
own free will around him, and from every corner come skirts
at full speed. While he collects himself a little, he discovers that
the disturbers of the peace are, when all is said and done, only
one person, and that's Sister. He tries to protest but is forcibly
silenced. "Quiet! Not a sound!"

Sister goes first to the telephone, then to Mother, then over to Katrine's door. She spins the dial furiously. "God, isn't anyone listening? Is it a wrong number again? Is this the doctor? This is Mrs. Kvam's. Something has happened here, all the pills are gone, I don't understand it, I had them in my breastpocket...yes, yes, almost, yes...oh God, thank you!" She feels Mother's pulse, her forehead and heart, then goes to Katrine's door again, pounds on it.

Here's Katrine. Or an incredible caricature of her, an ugly woman with pigtails down her back and a little puckered hole in her face where her mouth used to be.

Odd can't believe his eyes. Katrine has no teeth. She really has no teeth. Now and then she puts her hand in front of the hole in her face and tries to say something, but it sounds completely different than during the day, it doesn't even sound like speech. Is it really Katrine? No, it's not Katrine. Yes, of course it's Katrine.

She and Sister lift Mother over to the sofa and when the strange noise comes again from Katrine, Sister shouts, "Yes, yes, we can't bother ourselves about that now. An accident has happened here, can't you see? Please stay and help."

No one thinks about Odd. He is hidden in a corner. There he stands and can't take his eyes from the hole in Katrine's face.

The front doorbell rings violently. Katrine is already on the way, but then stops and stands there, turning around in the middle of the room with her hand in front of her mouth. Sister rushes past her and can hardly speak, she's so breathless. Tears trickle down. She repeats over and over, "I had them in my breastpocket. Here. In my breastpocket."

The doctor says nothing. With compressed lips and an angry face he starts in on Mother; he feels her here and there and tries to force a disgusting red rubber tube down her throat. Mother strikes out at the tube, closes her eyes and wants to be left in peace. They're mean to Mother, strict, angry, hard-handed. They've broken the telephone connection to Father. But if he doesn't come soon, there's no telling how it will end. Everything is painful and ugly and mean and crazy.

Something rubs against Odd's leg. He lifts up Puss, stands there with his arms full of Puss and suddenly gets the courage to start protesting as much as he can.

Stomping both legs and with the full power of his lungs so that everyone around him jumps, he bellows, "Call America, you have to call America. I won't stand for this any longer."

"Take the boy out, Katrine," says the doctor. "It's senseless for him to be here."

Odd is dragged out, howling and stomping, by the ugly, ugly Katrine, who isn't even Katrine.

He shrieks and shrieks.

From Katrine come new, incomprehensible sounds. But Katrine shouldn't be like this. No one should be like this, so ugly and wicked.

She pulls him over to his bed, lifts him up, covers him up and tries to say something.

Odd screams, kicks the covers off and shrieks. When Katrine tries to cover him again he kicks and hits her. Odd has never been so angry, so unhappy as long as he can remember. Nothing has ever been so horrible as it is now.

Katrine stands in the middle of his room with both hands in the air, speechless. If Odd even glances to the side, he sees her. She gets worse and worse to look at. When he finally gives up and is still, it's because there's no breath in him for more. Exhausted, he lies there and sniffles. But when Katrine tries to get near, to be nice and to comfort him, he strikes out at her again. That much he has strength for.

Suddenly Puss is there. Up there with him, with a hop, treading around as she does when looking for a good spot to lie down. Purring.

"Oh Puss, my Puss. You're so nice, Puss and *pretty*. You're pretty Puss, so pretty, never anything but pretty."

Odd folds his arms around Puss, presses his wet face down in Puss's fur. And without moving — extinguished by sorrow and rage, exhaustion and tears — he sleeps to the comfortable rumble of Puss, who purrs.

# The Art of Murder

FRANCINE ARRIVES.

I say, "Francine, you've come after all! You're not too tired then?"

"Oh no," answers Francine. "Not so I can't manage the washing up and children's clothes, Madame."

With that she bends her small, serious, early-faded, war-widow face over her tasks and gets to work. Francine has children to provide for. She works as househelp for the summer visitors and is paid by the hour. Besides, she is a sensible and dependable person who understands that when you're needed, you're needed.

Today we didn't expect her. She's covered eighteen kilometers, nine there and nine back, and been to a funeral. It wouldn't have surprised anyone if she hadn't returned to work. But now she stands here after all, rattling our plates.

The whole thing was unexpected. Someone came running, out of breath, over the meadows from the direction of the village shop where the telephone is. A relative of Francine's, a cousin, had died suddenly and was going to be buried this morning. Would Francine be able to come? "I suppose I'd better," said Francine, stopping her work a moment and considering, while scouring what she held in her hands even harder. When we asked her if she wouldn't rather quit for the day, go home and gather her thoughts a little, perhaps phone the house of mourning, she answered, "No thank you, that's not necessary." And we breathed a sigh of relief. We really do need Francine.

The messenger sat down by the kitchen door and caught his breath.

After a little while Francine turned to him and said, "It was Germaine, wasn't it? It wasn't the sister?"

"They said Germaine on the telephone."

"Good." Francine isn't someone who shows her feelings, either by words or by the expression of her face. Now she was plainly reassured. She almost looked pleased. It seemed a little strange, but Germaine was unmarried and the sister had several small children. Francine probably saw it from that perspective.

All the same it was a pity. I asked, "How did it happen, Francine? A young person like that?"

"Don't know, Madame. She died suddenly, according to what they say."

Francine pressed her lips together and I didn't want to ask more.

I've seen Germaine. I saw her last year. She came driving a cart full of apples for us from the people she worked for – rennet apples, big as children's heads, choice fruit without a spot, a hundred of them. Francine had arranged the purchase.

Germaine was a pretty girl with something gentle but also quite dispirited in her manner. She couldn't be persuaded to sit down, chat a little, drink a glass of cider. She helped us take the apples inside and then wanted to be on her way.

I said, "But she has to rest a minute. And what about the horse?"

"She'll rest the horse down by the bend," said Francine, who answered for the both of them. "She has acquaintances there." Germaine drove off and Francine explained, "She's shy and a little unsocial, Madame."

"But why? Such a pretty girl!"

"She's like that," said Francine and shrugged her shoulders.

Now she's buried. It's over with.

I should be content with that. Even Francine gives no sign

of being otherwise. Taciturn as usual, absorbed in her work. Yet I've *seen* Germaine, I remember her, however vaguely, and feel I should show my sympathy.

"It must have been hard for the parents, Francine."

Francine doesn't answer right away. Then she says, "Well, it was a daughter..."

"Yes..." I persist, slightly bewildered. And I come out with my thought about the children, using one of those cheap observations we have ready for these occasions, "But if something tragic had to happen — I mean, for the little ones' sakes..."

Francine turns her head a bit and looks at me with a small half smile, as if she finds me more than a little naïve. "She did leave a boy, Madame; she had one too. He's five years old."

That puts me in my place. It's not as simple and straightforward as it seems. She did leave a boy; she had one too. It may be worse in every way that this mother and not the other is gone. I've gotten myself into a muddle and had better keep quiet.

Whether or not she means to give me a clearer picture of the case, Francine says, "He's with her parents, naturally. Where else would he be? The father...? A foreign sailor, so we believe. Germaine took a trip to Lorient and then..."

And Francine shrugs her shoulders again.

"So she was out earning a living?"

"She had to, Madame. With a child to support. This last month she was home, though."

"Was she ill then?"

Francine smiles her half smile. It comes and goes so quickly that you can't be sure she really smiled. "Ill? If you want to put it that way, Madame."

An ambiguous answer. It must indicate that Francine is reluctant to talk about it. Well, there are certainly all sorts of illnesses. In order to say something I remark, "It's good, at least, that the boy has a home."

"Yes, of course," allows Francine. "It is." She opens her mouth to say more. Closes it firmly again as if, on thinking it over, she finds it better to be silent about certain things. The

situation definitely has a number of angles. It's easy to stand
outside, to say, "It's good, at least, that..." These people aren't
rich, even though they have a house and a little land, a couple
of cows and a pig. Francine, usually so uncommunicative, told
me that once. But they're not poor either. And Germaine
contributed to the boy's keep.

An intimate question slips from my tongue. Francine's
revelations are so strangely unsatisfactory that it would be better if she said nothing. "They do like him, Francine? The boy,
I mean? There at the farm?"

"They're not bad to him," answers Francine with reserve.

"Well, I should hope not."

"They're Christian people."

"Of course."

"It's not his fault."

"No, that's certain."

"But he's a bastard, isn't he? That's always a misfortune."

Francine is absolutely right. And words don't need to
mean more than exactly what they say. That it's a misfortune
to be a bastard, even for those who have a home, can't be
denied. But if you interpret them so that...interpret them so
that...

I wish I'd never gotten into this conversation with oracular
Francine. She has a tendency to express herself in double
meanings that can be taken many ways, just like those of
Delphi. It's all about a parentless little boy, a poor thing of five
years old, for whom you can't do anything. I get up to go.

Then Francine says — and she says it in an almost cheerful
tone, and without any intention of involving us in any drama,
"It was over quickly anyway. She did it herself."

"What? Did what?"

"She did it herself, Madame. She took her own life, as they
say."

"But good God, Francine — was she *so* unhappy?"

Francine has her own interpretation of the word unhappy.
She answers, "Oh no, Madame, she wasn't unhappy. But her
parents had told her that if it happened again, she'd just have

to manage it by herself with the first one and the other. And then..."

"And then, Francine? Had it happened? Was she...?

"Yes, Madame. It appeared that way."

I sit down again. Now I see Germaine plainly before me, remember things about her I didn't know I'd noticed. Pale, diffident, eyes frightened, an uncertain smile...

"But then she was unhappy, Francine."

"She wasn't unhappy, Madame."

"If neither her parents nor the child's father..."

"She only had to conduct herself properly. The rest of us do. She could have as well."

I have on the tip of my tongue that that's easy to say. I don't say it. Instead I ask about the child's father. Wasn't it possible to make him responsible this time either? It was his duty...

"Oh..." Francine rubs a plate, holds it up to the light and rubs anew, neat and conscientious. "It was an old man, Madame."

An old man. I'm dumb a second, then say, "Then he could have paid up in any case. If he was an old man."

"Somebody who'd been put away on the farm where she worked, Madame. An old man. They said he was always after her."

I don't know what more to say. I sigh, then I say, "Poor girl." And mean many things by that.

But Francine still has her own opinion and she is determined to make her point. "There was no reason to feel sorry for her, Madame. She could have behaved herself decently. We were all fed up with her because she couldn't behave herself decently. So when she got that way again and there already was a boy to raise...then...."

"So they were nasty to her."

"Not nasty. They said what they thought."

"She paid for her son, Francine."

"Not much. There was scarcely enough for one. If there had been two..."

"Now they have to support the boy alone," I say, pleased in a spiteful way.

"There could have been more, Madame. The way she was. And when she barely earned enough for one...."

Francine obviously feels on the side of the majority. She continues to stand there. No one stood on the dead woman's side. The icy breath of loneliness is all around her. She was one of the fragile vessels, perhaps one of those beyond saving. She probably would have ended up the way she did no matter what. It's hopeless to take on her case.

Once again, to emphasize the lighter side, Francine says, "It wasn't such a great loss, Madame. She had already started to act a little queer."

"What are you saying, Francine?"

"I'm saying she was a little strange lately. She didn't answer anymore if they spoke to her. It was like she didn't see people at all, like she was walking around in a daze. Her reason was almost gone, as they say. And when that's happened, it's almost better..."

Francine doesn't finish. What purpose would it serve? I should be able to understand the general family relief. Why pretend anything else? How much shame, how many expenses, how much stir is avoided now. It's only too reasonable that no one is crying.

But since details of this sort always have interest, Francine informs me, "She hanged herself. She tied a cord around her neck and hanged herself. It was to be expected, Madame. It was good she didn't throw herself in the well. They were afraid she might think of that. And a well.... It supposedly happened very quickly."

"It wasn't right in front of people?" I no longer know what I should believe and ask absurd questions.

"Oh no, oh no, Madame. Her mother had just turned her back on her. And then she went into the clothes closet. The door was half-way closed so no one heard it. But a few minutes later someone had to go in there and then they found her. She was already dead, so you see it was over quickly. They had

hung up clotheslines there, and she used them..."
I see. That I can't avoid. See above all a mother's back. Wide or narrow, going away and not turning. If it had...
I catch myself thinking that it's probably best as it is. She did what was most useful, what they expected of her. And she didn't throw herself into the well. She saw the cord in the storeroom, understood how it could be used...

"It wasn't such a great loss, Madame," says Francine once more. "When a person no longer has her reason..."

She calmly stacks the plates together and puts them back where they belong.

# To Lukas

*1940*

...I'M NO LONGER as good as dead, Lukas. Once in a while I'm alive. Then I catch myself believing that you're alive, too.

Half asleep in the evening, in dreams just before I wake, I feel your arms around me. In the middle of broad daylight you sit beside me on benches. It happens when I've been sitting for a long time. When the sun, warmth and drowsiness have loosened my bonds.

It began last summer. The numbness left me then, that awful sense of feeling nothing. It was then I began to see again, see myself and everything around me.

You know summer. Even here, so far north, its fragrance is overwhelming. From parks, from gardens, from unseen trees in flower. Like home, exactly like home. But here the nights are as light as a cloudy day where we come from. Sleep is almost impossible.

Not until late July did the evenings darken. After sunset the linden trees gave off fragrance. Like home. When I sat on the balcony after dinner I saw bats swooping long and soundlessly toward the twilight sky over the roofs. Lamps glowed in the open windows, pale stars came out, a couple of new ones every evening. A warm wind passed through the treetops down in the street, rustled the creeper vine on the wall, lifted up my skirt. It was so much like home then I could have screamed.

It was during that time you began to appear. Now you're

often here. You won't leave me in peace; I must try to explain myself.

I grew brave. Suddenly I grew brave. It bored him to sit on the balcony. None of the comfortable chairs would fit out there; he had to sit stiff as a rod on one from the dining room. I think he felt ridiculous. In this country they care a great deal about how they appear in other people's eyes. He wanted to listen to the radio and play solitaire. Me sitting on the balcony deck in the dark was something he didn't like.

He? Yes, he. But you needn't be jealous of him, Lukas.

I grew so brave that I went out on my own even though it was nighttime and not very considerate of me. He liked that even less. He took both acts as articles of a kind of declaration of independence. They were, too.

Once, when I went past him while he sat there playing solitaire, he said something about it being easy to go to the dogs.

Yes, I said. Really very easy.

It was said nastily. I owed him thanks, after all, I owed him respect.

Down in the street the pollen of linden flowers lay like old gold in the cracks between the cobblestones. The light wind leaves it behind everywhere. Like home. Like home there was music in the parks, music all around. There's water everywhere you look here; the city is built on islands. Under a couple of the bridges the current is swift; the eddies mirror the evening light; the sky is gilded behind the towers. Like the river at home.

They have a clock with chimes here, too. Not as sonorous as ours, not as much like an old-fashioned music box. The figures that come out aren't exactly the same — the Devil is absent, as is Death. You miss them, when you're used to them from childhood. They are part of life, the one as much as the other. All the same, the clock reminds me of home, so much that it makes me weak.

I sat down on a bench, listening to snatches of conversations about all kinds of harmless things — clothes, money, food, other people's relationships, little children. You'd think they have no idea what is happening in other countries, have no idea that there can be a banging on your door, that the police can stand there with guns in their hands when you open up, can tear your life into shreds in a second, taking your loved ones and forcing you out alone into the cold world. But perhaps we're all created so that we have to feel reality next to our bare skin before we can grasp it? Are we so lacking in imagination?

No, not everyone, but many. Most.

I often wish I understood less of the language here. But I haven't been able to avoid it.

On a bench one evening, something that had bound me burst – a hard shell that had grown up around me. I didn't cry. Crying is something no one does anymore. But I began to soften inside, the way we do when tears are close. I opened up, and you came. Out of the cold fog I'd been living in, I felt your warmth, I almost felt your touch. Along with all that seemed like home. You haven't left me since.

Thinking about how things can possibly be going for you, about how they've taken over at home and everywhere else, is something I have to put a stop to if I want to hold out. I have to block it from my mind, force the thought in another direction, the way I've involuntarily learned to do. Otherwise, a powerless anger comes over me like nausea; I want to scream, lash out, cause pain, create a scandal here in this calm, very respectable country.

At night I shove the thoughts away from me with both hands, thrusting against the dark as if against a wall I have to keep in place. So it won't come tumbling down and crush me.

Lukas! Lukas!


I'm no longer brave and you flee from me. You keep away as if to let me know that I'm cowardly, acting cowardly. But it's cold again, Lukas! Winter. Gray, bone-chilling winter.

Was out at the villa yesterday, where I stayed in the beginning. Refugees lived there even before the war, and some are still there. When I go there I dress in my old clothes.

They're not suitable for a polar expedition; I've usually gone there in mild weather. Yesterday I went in the freezing cold, under some kind of pressure to appear heroic probably, to make a good impression. You don't understand what I mean. You'll come to understand.

I suppose I wanted to see who was continuing to stick it out there. Whether perhaps all of them — how shall I say it — had given in to their inner weaknesses. Whether at least that little fair-haired one we called Miriam Hopkins* was gone. I think I hoped she was, as if that would raise me in my own estimation. Me? Miriam Hopkins *is* only a child.

Quite right, she was gone. No one knows where, not even the legation. Jan had been there to inquire. He detests going there, but had done it all the same.

Jan. He was one of the first who had to get away to a safe place, you know. (If you had only done the same, my God, if you had done the same.) We believed he was in England or in Holland, but he was here. He knows how things are, better than anyone, and shakes his head over Miriam Hopkins.

He, I say. He's a shadow of himself. By the time he arrived it was getting worse than before to be a refugee here. The students held a meeting and protested against the "importation of a foreign, intellectual work force." The students! I don't know why they are always assumed to be so liberal and free from prejudice. We must have made that assumption, to be so surprised later. But many a cautious, dry, repressed government official now in full flower was once a bud of a student, strangely enough.

Many took the refugees' side, but the protest still had its effect. Doctors got jobs as warehouse workers; art historians like K. — you remember K.? — got jobs washing dishes in restaurants. Jan got nothing. Maybe he didn't keep his eyes peeled, maybe he had his hands full keeping other people's spirits up. Maybe he was too proud.

Of all of us he is the one least capable of saying thanks,

*A film star popular in the 30s.

least capable of stretching out a hand to receive anything. He can't be won over by helpfulness – and good Lord, we've met with all sorts of helpfulness, you can hardly say otherwise. I think his opinion is that we were the shock troops that took the first blows for all the others, and that we shouldn't be treated like total beggars. But it's no use going around thinking that way, all of us know that.

He doesn't say much; his smile has become strange and distant. Occasionally we talk about you. In that careful way we have, over the last few years, grown accustomed to talking about close and like-minded friends. We almost speak in code, saying the same things over and over as if they were magic formulas. It's as though if we stopped talking about these things they'd cease to exist.

Rumors reach us. We winnow them still more cautiously. Now we're even afraid of our own countrymen.

In my time they'd found ways to manage out at the villa. It was warm there; we could read, write, sew, wash our clothes, steep our tea. This year there's no coal to be had, wood is rationed. It gets complicated for people like us; the most frequent result is that helpful people try to find us places by any means they can. We're afraid of those means. We don't act the way they'd like. It's often difficult for us to appreciate what they claim is for our own good. But they've won over some; Miriam Hopkins isn't the only one who's gone. Some people have understood their situation in the way they should, clearly and correctly. They have become the ideal refugees.

When I arrived they were sitting in the hall, where the only stove is. The villa is old-fashioned and only for summer use. But the kettle full of water that used to sit on the stove was gone. The water wouldn't have gotten very hot now anyway.

They were burning one of the garden benches. They have two left and will sacrifice one when the thermometer sinks a certain number of degrees below zero. They're considering going a little lower. It's obvious they don't get enough sleep.

Jan has a wool blanket he was persuaded to accept from an old lady he met in the street during last year's worst cold

spell. She went home and got it for him. The others have newspapers and their overcoats. I have a suspicion that Jan lets his
wool blanket make the rounds. He's unpleasantly blue and
skinny. If only the villa weren't empty. But it is empty and they
must be grateful; they might have had no villa at all. The old
actor who owns it said right away that *"fan"* had taken the
furniture (*"fan"* means the devil here), but that there were some
benches and a table under the veranda. For burning is probably
not what he meant, although Jan says that old actors aren't so
particular. They understand that kind of thing.

In my time Mirian Hopkins was the focal point. Was so
young, that's the funny thing about it. She came every morning
from a warm bed and sleep and breakfast. Lived in a good pension – after she left we used to bet on how long it would last.
She received money from the legation, may possibly have been
given it in a pleasant way, too, sweet and young as she was and
coming from the circumstances she did. But it didn't enable her
to live the way she used to, sitting around in restaurants every
single evening and going without work.

Her coat billowed with blue fox around the elbows. In a
totally superfluous spot, so anyone could see it was a whim of
fashion and the purest luxury. When the cold grew severe, we
advised her to take the fur off and put it around her neck, but
Miriam Hopkins wasn't the type who can sew and alter. She
didn't want anyone to help her do it, either; she was insulted
and wounded by the whole idea, full of defiance. A tiny little
hat cocked over one eye, pumps, silk stockings, painted mouth.
That was the fashion the winter of '38, for those who could get
themselves things that were slightly expensive, not too ordinary, and who could go out, fired with warmth from a warm
home.

When she took off her shoes in the villa, cold and wet from
walking through the snow from the streetcar, we saw she had
large holes in the soles. Some helpful man was always on hand
to take the shoes from her and set them over by the stove.
Helpful men lined her path. But carrying her shoes with the

soles turned down was something they never thought of.

She sat down, rubbing her frozen stiff, pretty child-feet, unable to camouflage the fact that her stockings were finished, too. They were bunched together in a number of places under her feet, so that the darning on the heel wouldn't be visible over the shoe. A very young person's short-sighted concern for outward appearances. She sat there grimacing as life began to return to her feet, looking like Miriam Hopkins.

It wasn't such a good thing, that resemblance. Everywhere she went there was someone who stared at her. With a distant look, untouchable, ladylike, she gazed past the individual, very much the sort who receives her proper homage where she should and doesn't need to collect it in the streets and markets. But alone in her room, with her coat hanging inside her closet and all the day's possibilities behind her she was, in spite of the warmth, the bed, the food and the single room, nothing but a tired, wronged child with an alarmed and perhaps frightened face. It was easy to see why. It's far from easy to resemble a film star, to have dreamed of being one, and in reality to be a silly little girl, pulled up by your shallow roots and slung haphazardly out into the harsh world.

You say perhaps that Miriam Hopkins was surely no political figure of any importance. I wasn't one, either; no one needed to be. Jan explains that her father was involved in business on a large scale and wasn't at their beck and call when he should have been. They took him and all he had. Miriam Hopkins came here with the help of friends. Later they had themselves to worry about; no one can blame them for that.

Jan is worried about her, can't get used to the fact that she doesn't come to the villa any longer; he talks about solidarity among countrymen and about going to look for her. But what can he do, he who looks like a ghost from hunger and rootlessness and whose clothes have become so bizarre that he doesn't wear shoes inside his rubber boots, just white socks. Wool socks that he's traded for some other clothes and that he can't manage to keep even passably clean. The kindest people would be frightened of someone like him.

Work? A job for Miriam Hopkins? She can't do anything but what a spoiled little bourgeois girl can do, one who's always had servants around her at home and hasn't even graduated from high school. As a rule that's not much.

She could take care of children, couldn't she? Jan thinks. Take care of children, wash dishes in a restaurant, fell trees in the woods, all of it for a ridiculous wage — that's what refugees are limited to in a foreign country. She didn't want to do any of those things; the woods were totally out of the question. She didn't want to type for the legation, either, nor to become the useful and comforting companion of some respectable old lady.

The worst was that she didn't want to move out of the pension. She clung to it, even though any day she could have been evicted for unpaid bills.

No, no doubt the worst was that she'd been an extra in a couple of films during the first period here. In some worthless publicity films. Who in the world would have dragged her along to the so-called film town?

She wouldn't allow herself to be evicted; it wasn't hard to figure out why, either. Blindly and at the last minute she would allow someone to "fix things" for her, someone who could pay. Those who plan on a future in films must live in such and such a way, she would explain; you had to frequent restaurants, keep in touch with people.

From no point of view was she the way a refugee should be.

I'm not either, Lukas, I'm not either.

If a decent husband had only come in time, Jan said about Miriam Hopkins. If only she hadn't been thrown out in the world so alone, eighteen years old, going on nineteen.

You could actually see the man before your eyes the way Jan imagined him: a businessman, well off, well dressed, spruce and confident.

As if, in these times, it always helps to have a man.

A slick gentleman, who knew how to trim his sheets to the wind, was what Jan must have meant. When it comes to Miriam

Hopkins, I believe he's capable of a surprising political tolerance. Intellectually, at any rate.

Poor Jan. That shortsighted child had become a warmth, a sort of modest renewal in his desolate life. A romantic, we used to call him, but who from home could he go around missing? Nothing ever came of him and his old flame. He was just the victim for a Miriam Hopkins. And now he's freezing like all the rest of us.

And me? Was I relieved because she was gone? Did I feel rehabilitated? As if I too were a child? I'm not one, definitely not.

Why am I telling you so much about her? Is it to avoid talking about myself for a while? In the long run I still can't escape an explanation.

When they ask me where I'm staying I say something about a post with an old widower. But he's not old, he's never been married and I haven't so much as set the table or watered a flower in his house. So now you know, Lukas.

My opinion is that he's never really known any women. That probably sounds strange, since he's at least forty, but they're different from us here. You can't imagine how repressed and strange they are. Except when they've had a little alcohol. Then they get uproariously boisterous, whack each other on the back and call each other brother. They get poetic, sometimes so much so that they want to touch you a little, too. They couldn't be less dangerous. You feel a little sorry for them. It's as if they were trying to break out of a shell without finding a way. Falling in love is impossible here, I think, however young and easily inflamed you might be. As impossible as, for example, in Germany. Here, as there, people look too satisfied.

You're probably asking, why him instead of somebody else, instead of the first man on the street to come along.

I felt I knew him a little. I wasn't afraid of him. Most likely my idea was that I could hold my own against him until something else turned up. Being a refugee doesn't make you nice, Lukas.

\*

To write to someone, not knowing whether he's alive or where he is – surely, many people have done this before me? In times of war and violence? Those in captivity, those who were taken off as slaves – didn't they sit down sooner or later and scratch something on a leaf, if nothing else, or on a stone? Putting hope in time and chance? The way a sailor does when he throws a bottle with a letter in the sea?

Am I writing about insignificant things? No, about significant things. About what we would have talked about when everything irrelevant had been said. Don't turn away from me, don't judge me. You can't judge. Anyway, you know as well as I do that when the devil really wants to make a mess of a person's life, he lets them freeze. That nothing paralyzes like the cold.

No, I said, no and no and no. Then I said yes. It was twenty-six degrees below freezing that day. I didn't have winter clothes. I had that black suit of mine, a mere summer suit. And I'd been evicted.

Language classes? I tried all right. That's the first thing you think of. Those who help refugees would be willing to help me, too. When I mentioned language classes, they shrugged their shoulders. No one here studies our language, least of all now; our country has been obliterated. There are lots of teachers of other languages. People have stopped taking language classes, anyway; they're withdrawing.

I took the job they found for me.

Could I have stuck with it longer? I got so tired, Lukas. Healthy twins between the age of two and three are taxing. I never fell asleep before dawn. By then they were already up, running around the apartment, turning on the gas in the kitchen, getting hold of matches, making puddles on the waxed floors. All that it was my job to prevent. But I slept. Eventually I slept so that I never even heard them. A lot of things happened that shouldn't have.

I was hardly grateful enough either, in spite of thirty-five kroner a month and everything free. They expect a lot of gratitude from us foreigners.

I lived for three weeks in a hotel, on money enough for one week. I felt like a trapped animal in my room. Only when the corridor was empty, when I knew the hotelkeeper wasn't sitting behind her desk, did I sneak out. But I had to come in again, too. Sometimes I walked for hours outside in the cold.

The villa? Didn't I have the villa the same as the others? I'm not much of a hero, Lukas. I wanted warmth night and day, warmth and rest. I'm demanding, I refuse to accept conditions any worse than absolutely necessary.

The afternoon I was threatened with the police and with being put out on the street, I went to him and said yes. I compromised my principles.

Should I have looked for a new job as soon as possible? What would you have liked me to say when those kind people asked me what could I do, what had I done before in my life? That I was my beloved's pride and joy, his model and his critic? That I have a certain understanding of art, can arrange flowers and interiors nicely, make an omelette, darn stockings? They were sitting there waiting; they let me collect my thoughts, while they tapped with a pencil on the tabletop. They seemed prepared for anything. But they would be impatient with that answer, Lukas; they would shrug their shoulders and return to the idea of taking care of children and dishwashing.

With people like me there's not much to be done. We probably lack the right attitude, the refugee attitude, the humility.


The children are sleeping, Ma'am. They ate their mush, they went potty. Am I allowed to go out, Ma'am?

I remember myself standing there, saying that. A little too often perhaps, but the arrangement was that I had leave to go out now and then while the children were sleeping.

The mother hesitated. Today again? When you've just this moment come from the park with the youngsters? Not too long then, remember the underwear.

In reality I never forgot the underwear; it never happened that the children lacked a clean change. But sometimes I stood over the laundry until late in the evening. I should have been finished earlier and satisfied with my hour in the park.

I went down to the café. Even in good weather I had my umbrella with me. We grow so odd, Lukas, so different. Before, I loathed dragging along unnecessary things, especially umbrellas. But this was the only new thing I owned, a rather coquettish umbrella. When I put it down on the table next to my purse and gloves, I imagined that it contributed to an impression of being well dressed. My clothes didn't get any nicer from taking care of children, you know. Black, especially, gets a little shabby.

It was good to settle down at the little table next to the sunny wall, lean against it, light a cigarette and wait. Around me and over me flickered the leafy shadows of the trees, thinner day by day. Day by day they became more blue against the wall and the sand. You know how transparent the light is just on those last mild fall days, how light the shadows, how unreal and far too beautiful it all is.

They noticed me from the counter inside. I heard the pale, dark-haired waiter come slowly across the floor, heard his steps continue over the gravel.

A cup of coffee, a small pastry, together it came to thirty-five øre plus ten as a tip. Strangely enough, it all adds up if you spend that much every day. We thought we were stretched thin lots of times, you and I, and that we managed well with the little we had. We were rich, Lukas. We were never in a position where we had to count out one and two øres. A person comes quite near that with thirty-five kroner a month, even when she has free board, if she's arrived in this country with no luggage except two of your rolled up canvases. On the boat I kept them under my clothes so they wouldn't get wet.

Sell them, you say. No, Lukas.

It wasn't the coffee that mattered; it was terrible, anyway. It was that the time was my own. It was me sitting there – at any rate the shadow was mine. She who bent her back over the children's washing and took care of two wild children and couldn't really manage either thing was someone completely different. Someone belonging to the new nation, the nation above nations. Or under them, whichever way you see it. Who could be from anywhere.

I didn't notice him at first; he's not like that. Ordinary, neither thin nor fat, neither blond nor dark. Quite ordinary. He read the paper, smoked, tossed crumbs to the birds. He wasn't there every time, either.

Then it became every time. But there was nothing peculiar about *that*. Nor that one day he politely directed a few words to me. You come here often, too, Madame? Pleasant little place as long as the weather holds. It'll be winter soon. Pleasant to sit here in the sun.

Yes, very pleasant.

There wasn't a great deal more then. I'm not talkative, you know; he's even less so. There wasn't much more I could say in the language at that time either.

When he speaks of his loneliness, I feel the way I can imagine a horse feeling, when someone for the first time tries to coax a bit into its mouth. I resist with aversion. But sympathy is a tender spot inside us, a spot that can be steered from as if with a bridle. I've heard that in North Africa they keep wounds open constantly on their beasts of burden, wounds they poke when directing the animals one way or another.

Now is the time when the lonely see their chance and take it; they'd be stupid not to. Those who no one thought were amusing, who weren't destined to win anyone's heart. Some of them assail us with sympathy, others with gratefulness; both of them feel like skinless, stinging spots. They win us over with simple things, the kind of things you think should be everyone's unequivocable right. They bind us with bonds that quickly cut into the flesh. The down and out are easy to bind; in the midst of a bad time they let themselves be led to the yoke, obedient as cows and just as blind. Like birds under a hat we can be caught, if only the moment is right. And the temperature.

Lonely people and practical people. For we've become utensils, Lukas, that lay around and can be gathered up. We're like spoons or forks someone has lost or thrown away, and that should be made use of.

Nasty? Certainly I'm nasty. We haven't grown kind. I'm unjust too, toward some, toward some few.

No, I said when we suddenly bumped into each other on the street one day and I had lived in the hotel almost three weeks and had begun to look different than during the fall at the café.

I said no to "temporarily lodging with him," as he put it.

The next day I went there and said yes. That's sensible, he said. I'm pleased.

We went out and ate dinner together, a nice, hot dinner; as much food as I wanted, wine. Just the smell of food and wine, just the thick warm air made me numb, even a little drunk. But nothing happened, no word fell that could bar the road, or frighten me. It would have taken something extraordinary.

I sat there, mortified by my black suit that looked so threadbare and poor, and I never really got warm inside. But I had a respite from numbness anyway.

When I came back to the hotel I went right in, right past the desk where the hotelkeeper herself sat. The gaze that followed my back didn't penetrate. If she'd said anything, I could have answered, Get the bill ready for tomorrow, thank you.

The day after, I moved. Settled up and moved. He came and fetched me by car. What they thought in the hotel I could give "*fan*" for, as they say here. They probably thought as he did, that I was "sensible." Besides, money always arouses respect, I've never known it not to. Now more than ever before.


He turned to me in the doorway. Do you think you'll be happy here?

I said, Yes, thanks very much. It's certainly — it's splendid here.

He left. So I could fix myself up a bit, rest. I probably

looked like I needed it, and he is a well brought up person.

As he was leaving he smiled slightly, a smile that caused me pain and made me turn watchful. It was meek, perhaps disappointed. I had, after all, said almost nothing. He probably thought he could have expected more.

But behind everything else in that smile lay confidence. The confidence that came of knowing he had many resources on his side.

I acted differently toward him after that — stiffer.

I stood and stared at the bed. At the time I didn't have the means, nor the energy, to see it as it was, an insult. Far too wide, far too luxurious; resplendently, horribly new, covered with silk and down, and over that a lace spread. Without really seeing it, I stared, while a tough little hard kernel of attentive resistance began to knot up deep inside me. The main thing was to take without being fleeced myself.

Otherwise I didn't absorb many details just then, no more than that the whole thing resembled a display window in a so-called better furnishings store. Over the arm of an easy chair lay the quilted, salmon pink dressing gown that's never missing in such windows; slippers of the same color were placed on the floor. On the night table was a book with uncut pages that fit with the whole thing.

The kind of interior stupid little ladies wish for, standing in front of the plate glass windows. It's horrible here, I thought; it's expensive, tasteless and disgusting. Viewed as a trap it's idiotic, it sounds an alarm from far away. You really have to pity the man.

And simultaneously: It's lovely here, it's warm. It's not costing a cent.

Remember what I'd come from, Lukas.

I stood feeling cozy warmth awaken me. Since I wasn't going out again, it penetrated inside. You know how that feels, when you've had frost-bitten fingers and life slowly comes back into them. It aches. I ached all over.

I could see myself in the large mirror. It had been a long

time. You don't often come across a mirror where you can see your whole figure, once you've become a rolling stone. They are, in fact, few and far between, Lukas.

It was like watching someone wake from the dead. First I was cloudy blue, with blue lips; my body was stiff and constrained. Then, little by little, the color of life came back, and my limbs loosened up in movement.

You always said I looked like a Toulouse-Lautrec, that mine was the 1880s style. You preferred me in black, for my green eyes and my reddish hair. Just the faintest bit depraved, you might say, and be in love with me because of it.

I knew well what I was worth, you said. I didn't deny it. I admitted to myself as well that until you came along I had calculated coldly and clearly. Along with the picture of me in the mirror came memories that seemed from another life, another world. Of that chic poverty of ours, with the nice inexpensive things we'd painstakingly chosen. You were in them, distant and shadowy, but that's just when I had to turn away from you.

I was back to that cold, clear way of calculating again, that much I knew.

*Because I want to be like before, when we meet, Lukas. Don't want to have become old and worn out and ugly, do you hear! That's the point of view from which you must judge everything I'm letting happen to me.*

Twenty-six degrees below. I didn't know where you were or even if you were alive, don't know to this moment. No one spoke of our country any longer. Now it was other countries, neighbors to this one. We take the hand that is extended, are glad to be allowed into the warmth.

That's the first and most important thing. Warmth in all forms. Simple wisdom we didn't consider during peacetime. Now we have it pounded into us the hard way.

Why do I tell you this? If you're alive you probably know it better than I do. This winter is a terrible one all over Europe, from what we hear. As if everything else weren't enough.

God's wrath — do you remember how I used to laugh at such
expressions? I said, If he exists, what is he so angry for? He
made us the way we are himself.

You said I was a sweet little silly philosopher, who was
probably right.


I felt as if I were in a film, an absurd comedy, when I was
awakened that first morning with tea and newspapers by Mrs.
Sjøkvist, the housekeeper, and was helped into a bedjacket of
quilted satin, that insistently crude fabric of the nouveau riche
and the demimonde. Yet another of those garments that sales-
ladies fool inexperienced men into buying.

There I lay, chewing toast and reading the horrible news
that never comes to an end, that only gets worse and worse.
But the warmth around me, the soft bedclothes, the wide bed
where I could lay sideways if I wanted, were like an anesthetic,
making everything distant.

Someone who has saved herself on a reef, while others are
in the sea, perhaps has a similar feeling.

The bath, Lukas, when I got up and all there was to do
was to go in and turn on the hot tap, can't possibly be described.

When you finally read this you'll be free and will have
taken a bath yourself. Otherwise I would never have mentioned
it.

In the beginning I wandered around the apartment as if
lost.

There was a smell of tobacco and some sort of hair tonic
in the room they call the study. The tobacco was good, the hair
tonic more doubtful.

In there were his books, the country's classics and thick
bestsellers in English. It never occurred to me to sit down in
there, nor in what they call the parlor, either. I poked around
in the bookshelves until my model room was straightened up,
took a book with me and went back in again. Or out.

Not often. I wasn't dressed for it. The cold kept up; it felt
like an anesthetic. One that paralyzed me so that I could only

think of one thing, getting back to the warmth again. An ordinary man, not in himself dangerous, who conducted himself correctly, with a certain chivalry. And I was *freezing*. Every time I was out, I thought, You're not obliged to go back. But I had no other place to go. The legations, you say. The legations have become dispensers of charity, Lukas; no one seeks charity if they can avoid it. After a short walk I was back in my room again, gratefully accepting Mrs. Sjøkvist's offer of a warm cup of tea.

But who is kind without expecting something in return? Not many. We don't get something for nothing in this world. If I hadn't learned the lesson before, I learned it now; it impressed me as much as the one on warmth.

There was something in the air from the first moment. The bed if nothing else shrieked it. For a long time I thought, I don't need to let on that I understand. That sort of expectation can be kept at a distance, inasmuch as it's tactless to draw certain conclusions.

But when things have, to no purpose, been in the air a while, even the timid take the offensive. One day there was a fur coat hanging in my closet, *petit gris* and my size, exactly what you so much wanted to give me and never could. It seemed like sorcery, for on one count you must believe me; I've never hinted at such a thing. It hasn't reached that stage yet.

I didn't touch the coat, just closed the closet door. I couldn't help but think of bait put out for a starving animal. I felt a little nauseated and for the first time thought seriously of escaping, of going back to the villa, of confiding in Jan.

I knew all too well what he'd tell me.

And I didn't go.

Later that day, when I came in from outside in my black suit and naturally was blue in the face and frozen stiff, he stood in the entry way. He looked embarrassed and bewildered; I think he was waiting for me. He stammered a little as he said, But — didn't the coat fit? Wasn't it your style? In that case it can be exchanged. Shall we go and exchange it this afternoon?

It's far too elegant. I've never worn a fur coat. I'd like you to please return it.

He got furrows around his mouth, didn't answer right away. After a while he said, This is an unusually severe winter. All the women I see are wearing fur coats. I meant to do something nice for you.

I had to answer that I understood that.

Nothing came out of it, no discussion. It wasn't a matter for discussion, either. That was obvious to each of us.

The coat remained hanging there, but was never mentioned again.

Once more I felt sorry for him. He plays with an open hand. And I do not.


I had thought, he said one day, that we would become friends.

We are friends.

Are we? You don't trust me.

Don't I? I live in your house.

There was nothing he could say to that. I knocked his weapon from his hand, I think. We talked of something else.


War, war, war everywhere.

Here they complain about the food, about more and more things being rationed, about the rations themselves.

Mrs. Sjøkvist says, How is it going to turn out? What will we live on in the end? All the children we're taking in, all the people we have to support? It's wonderful that we can do what we're doing, that's for sure. A little country like us. There are kind people here, no one can say otherwise. But some day when we have nothing ourselves, who's going to help us?

I answer, Yes, Mrs. Sjøkvist. No, Mrs. Sjøkvist. I agree with Mrs. Sjøkvist. For strangely complicated reasons. A little out of scorn, mostly out of tiredness, because I believe it's useless to contradict her, because there's nothing to object to. She's right; they *are* kind. They could have refrained from doing anything at all. That wouldn't have looked good, but... There's something they don't understand, don't take into account. Exactly what, I can't be sure. It's something about — something about the shock troops, those on the front line. Those who are sacrificed.

Miriam Hopkins works in a beauty parlor.

One day, when I went by chance into a new place to get my hair done, she suddenly stood before me, as if she'd shot up out of the ground. Embarrassed at first, then self-assured in the anxious manner you might have expected. Parrying from the first moment. She was well dressed, well coiffed, quite changed, far too hurriedly matured, chic in her white smock.

The profession of beautician is one of the few open to foreigners, she explained, without my having asked anything. They lack skilled workers.

It probably wasn't so odd that she mentioned it. She can justifiably be proud of taking care of herself. It just came out too quickly and sounded too much like set phrases she'd rattled off many times, using them as a defense.

Training? It would have been kinder of me not to ask about it, more tactful. But I got the answer, friendly and unreserved. Someone in the pension had loaned her money, an older gentleman who wished her well. She had an apartment, two rooms, bath, telephone, a little dog. Wouldn't I visit her? Call first, to make sure she was home.

She scrutinized me with appraising, experienced eyes when she thought I wasn't looking. Her friendliness was the kind you show someone in the same situation.

But surely I'm not sitting in judgement of Miriam Hopkins?

Me? Paragon of virtue who takes without giving the compensation I know very well was the price? And expose both you and me to unworthy suspicion?

I found out a great deal I didn't know. For Miriam Hopkins goes to cafés the evenings she's alone. Cheap places, reeking of tobacco smoke and noise, where refugees gather. She has no reason to hide. She's done well for herself, earns her keep and doesn't cheat anyone.

She said that Jan continues to live in the villa and that he looks miserable; his clothes hang on him, patched and disgusting. Sometimes he washes dishes in a restaurant, but even such work is difficult to get, now that there are refugees from so many countries here. He's not aggressive about getting work, either; usually he lets others go before him. He often sits in libraries, manages that way. It's warm there, and you can stay far into the evening.

He's really impossible, said Miriam Hopkins. He *wants* to suffer, he really does. And what a schoolmaster he is. It's almost as if we're betraying our country when we're just making the best of the situation.

You have to be reasonable, she said sagely.

I thought, He's the most honest of us all, the proudest and best.

He is the only one of your old friends I've met here; he's the closest to me. But he wouldn't let me help him, I know that, even though I have a "salary" now and could easily do it. Everything must have a name. The bills that once a month are placed on my table in an envelope are called a "salary." Oh yes, I put flowers in vases, do it with more flair than Mrs. Sjøkvist, make up a menu now and then, go out occasionally and choose a new lampshade or a sofa cushion. I couldn't go on forever asking for money to buy a toothbrush, Lukas; I accepted it. I accepted that, too.

If I were to meet Jan and explain the situation to him, he would be friendly, perhaps cordial; he wouldn't be the sort to judge or believe the worst. But he would disapprove of me and he wouldn't let me help him. I could get down on my knees and beg as if for a favor. I feel cut off from my people because of him, and perhaps I deserve it.

Otherwise, everything is turning out well, as they say, for

most of them. There are those who seem quite satisfied, says Miriam Hopkins. Certain intellectuals' wives, for example, go around glowing like new brides. They've gotten their husbands placed in steady jobs: restaurant kitchens, warehouses, offices, in the best cases. They live in small, dingy rooms, eat badly and cheaply, struggle and slave away with washing and house-keeping. But they have their husband the way they haven't had for a long time. He's finally in their possession, cut off from any chance of sitting in cafés day and night like before, drinking, arguing, spending too much and being irritable at home. Now he goes back and forth at set times; at the most he goes out on Saturday.

Some women sometimes lose their bearings to the extent that they get married, legally, quickly and for all the wrong reasons. They want to become citizens here, probably longing for what women do long for: their own home, protection. Miriam Hopkins considered it a rash act, with justification. Tying themselves down, was how she put it. Surely one fine day we'll be going back?

I'm not that stupid, she said.

Personally I never go where I can meet my own people. I go elsewhere.

On the sidewalks, outside the cafés and restaurants, it smells like fat frying. A smell that turns your stomach. It probably smells like that all over Europe, anywhere they still have something to eat.

So many nationalities are in exile now that I can't keep track of them. The languages buzz in your ears. And life has become naked, Lukas, bitterly naked, exposed and without privacy.

If only we could be together at night they say, for anyone to hear; if only we could have the night together. They live wherever they can, usually in separate places.

Human intimacies are tossed out carelessly. To listen is like having your clothes ripped off. If you so much as poke your head outside the shelter you've found, a wind immediately starts blowing that can rip it off.

People from the neighboring countries come from their legations, white-faced and with the devil's name on their lips. If I go inside and drink coffee — what they're calling coffee now — I hear them at the next table. And I understand what they say because I understand the language here. The differences are so slight.

"*Fy fanden*," they say, talking about the lady at the legation they've been visiting to get money from.

"*I fandens skinn og ben*," they say and mean the devil's skin and bones.

It's possible to travel via Tibet, they assure each other. If you just have a gun, you'll manage. The road through Tibet....

They intend to go to England. Everyone wants to go there; they're prepared to travel around the world to get there. In England they'll avoid living on charity; they'll be put to use again and feel like free men. Many of them fought, when there was still armed resistance.

The disbursement of money is an odd thing, Lukas. It doesn't matter how much it's the right of the recipient nor how little it's the property of the one who's paying. But the latter seldom denies himself the gift of making it seem like benevolence, alms-giving and charity. It's a powerful feeling to sit behind the desk of the director of charity. Arrogant nobodies from the neighboring countries sit there now, puffed up with importance and good incomes, in positions established for them. They arouse bitterness.

Otherwise, I have to admit that many things have improved. The country's helpful people have come up with all sorts of solutions, have gotten organizations going, workers' camps, homes; they've made it possible to get training. I have no excuse any longer, I could have learned something long ago. I could have stood on my own two feet just as well as Miriam Hopkins, on sturdier feet than hers.

Or is it that I want, above all else, to be young and radiant and lovely when you and I meet?

The force of habit is also strong. Here I am going on the second year....

1942

A night in June with a slight wind. A moon. Rosebushes in bloom, a whisper of leaves, a fragrance of hay. And you near me. Like last year, like the year before that. This is your landscape; you've chosen it like spirits choose the midnight hour. The memory of our summers still stays with me like a fizzing in the blood. Can two people be happier than we were?

Come. Keep coming. Don't take away my belief that you're alive, that we will find each other again, that the evil will be as if obliterated. It's such a fragile hope, Lukas. It flickers, sometimes flattens completely, like a flame without nourishment. In winter, the eternal winter, it's barely a spark in the ashes, often not even that. A dead place.

If I were to lose it for good, I don't know what would become of me. To allow everything to drift, allow things to drift to their final conclusion, just for the sake of material well being, for the sake of security, warmth and food, for peace and stability — that temptation isn't foreign to a refugee. You must understand, feel it yourself, wherever you are; you mustn't give up on me, Lukas. Nor break into my thoughts as you sometimes do, as if just to tell me that everything is finished and in vain, that maybe we wouldn't even recognize each other again, because we've changed so much.

I am the same. Not for others, but for you. If you came now, the experienced, calculating refugee mentality would slip off me like the shape of the enchanted one in the fairy tales. Your shape would fall from you and the enchantment would be lifted.

But you must hold me by the hand. I'm holding you....

*

I became ill, was ill for a while, don't really know myself with what or for how long. I started vomiting, then lost consciousness. When it was over I was tired, passive and obedient. Books, presents and flowers were laid on my bedspread. I accepted everything and thanked him with a handshake like a little girl. I believe I thought it was a good thing to do. Knowing the whole time that I was once again going further than was honest and than I wanted. Necessity is one thing; excess another.

There were the rumors. Suddenly they were worse than ever and more than I could stand. Newspapers that refer to them aren't allowed to circulate in the country. Sometimes they're suppressed and the editor arrested. It's called neutrality.

The rumors pinch you like tongs. They're like what they talk about, damaging body and soul, violating all human dignity. If they're true, an execution is nothing in comparison, is something brief and clean.

In spite of everything, I'm unable to wish that you were dead. But I often wish we both were. That we'd been laid in the earth together during a time when we could still hope to die decently. Why did you get me to promise that I would escape if they took you? If you're dead, I could have been too by now.

More than rumors reach us. People from a neighboring country come here to bear witness with their injuries, to show the world what is happening.

The world lets anything happen, I guess.

Some of them are simple people, the kind who haven't learned a lot, yet still know the difference between right and wrong, often better than the learned and the great. And take the consequences. Their open, slightly credulous faces are what you see in front of you, thinking the word fatherland. They are the very foundation it's built on.

I don't see you, I *feel* you. At rare times that are both my best and worst, you still come and I feel your warmth, your touch. In an unexpected and blessed dream we can, in spite of all the horror, be tender and close together.

All the same, not long ago, just after the illness when I'd awakened from a nap, you sat on the side of the bed and looked at me, a little mischievously, the way you used to when I overslept. Indescribably relieved and happy I stretched out my arms to you. But you were gone. I sat there holding them out, and they were empty.

Ten men shot today in P.
Sixteen men in B.M.
Twenty yesterday in S.
The whole provincial town of L. razed to the ground, the men shot, women and children taken away to an unknown place.

This isn't something out of horror novels, nor something made up by my crazed mind. It's not soldiers in battle, but peaceful civilians.

It's in the newspapers and is read aloud on the radio. Without commentary, neutral. Not as dangerous to neutrality, oddly enough, as the rumors I mentioned the other day. A puzzling concept.

Every time it has to do with our country he puts flowers in my room. Nice of him. Today it's chrysanthemums, the season's bloom, the only kind obtainable.

He can't know, of course, that you and I always thought they smelled of the grave.

*Who* they've shot we may find out months later. Through the Red Cross. Maybe. It's anything but certain.

I've taken out my fur coat again. It's chilly and since I ended up wearing it last year without resistance...

It's wonderful to touch, wonderful to wrap around myself. It burns my body. I long to run away with it, rescue it from all that — of my own free will — entraps me.

Of my own free will?

He gets far too smug when he sees it hanging in the entry way. That's sensible, he says. It could get cold any time now.

It's the same when I am the hostess for his strange, stiff

friends. Those who toast each other so solemnly and never toast me, but who do, however, make short speeches to me. A couple of them are married; that hasn't changed them. I never see their wives, whether it's because they can't be shown off or because I can't. Probably me. It's so peculiar in this country that one can be invited without the other, and not even the husband is offended.

Or when I've redecorated the rooms a bit and he has to admit that things really do look better. He doesn't say much afterwards; in general he never says much. But he hums and is in a good mood. And for a time I grow cautious.

I shouldn't act that way. It leads to misunderstandings. The air can be so heavy with them that I sometimes have to say something short and almost heartless.

But it's not easy to go around like this in a home month in and month out the way I do. It's unnatural and brings its own punishment. Gratitude is a force, has a warmth of its own and sweeps you along, not least when it's mixed with guilt. Habit is another. Terror of being miserable again the third and most insidious. Nor is it possible for a woman to go around seeing that things are in the wrong places. Not for long. It makes her uneasy. It makes her hands and her soul itch.

If he were different than he is, I could certainly go farther than I do. Not from desire, not from love. From loss.

Two arms around me when night comes, Lukas, that long night that seems not to want to receive the lonely, but closes cheerfully and willingly around those who are two; I can miss that so much I feel stiff and frozen through as if by frost. And dry and old as wood.

Yet the rare times you come to me in dreams, I thank Providence that they are the way they are, the men I meet. Not unlikeable, no, dignified, not what you'd call fat either, only too well fed, too unimaginative. It's as if centuries of secure conditions had made them heavy in both body and soul.

I want to save myself for you, want it like the first day I saw you.

*

*1943*

The sound of heavy soldiers and boots reaches me from the street. Here too they're marching. I think, They are neutral, they're going out to drill, not to war, for them it's easy enough. Just the same, I feel sorry for them, for they should have been doing something else, too, something they liked perhaps, and they had to leave it in order to go out marching. Their boots have a desolate, barren sound. As if they laid waste the earth.

Last night I dreamed that old dream of not measuring up. It returns again and again in the course of my life, in different forms.

I was packing and packing. The hour of departure neared. I suddenly remembered that my things were spread out all over the place; I wouldn't have time to get them together. There I stood, putting things in and taking them out again, totally confused.

Later in the dream there was someone who caressed my breasts. But they had become tiny, rockhard balls of something like old rubber, without sensation. I cried. I felt the world was dead, if my own breasts were dead, where the child would be looking for nourishment and the man looking for peace. Now they were dead. Someone laughed somewhere, a little hunchback who sat at a table, teetering on his chair. I realized I knew him from long ago, but couldn't make out who he was.


I can't stand it any longer. I must leave.

He's begun to say "we." A new, quiet little chess move and not a minor one. One that means it's getting to be about time, that even inexhaustible patience has its limits and that claims are made to be cashed in. I take care to act as if I haven't heard.

I'm tired of holding my own against him, tired of his eyes, of gifts and friendliness, of things that hang in the air. He's choking me with all of it.

An inexplicable man, you say, perhaps. A man who's not a man?

Yes, he is, Lukas; it's just that he's not brutal but, in his way, chivalrous. He could have barred the door a long time ago. Or else he could have said, What do you actually think you're here for, my dear lady?

He continued to wait. He's one of the waiters, Lukas, the timid, silent, eternally patient waiters. It's their moment now too, not just the down and outers.

The woman probably hasn't been born who won't, sooner or later, run into them. The no-longer-young men without experience, who follow her unswervingly with their eyes and get stronger through their constant waiting. You could easily shake them off when the necessities of life weren't at stake. They had almost no chance. Now...

You see, they can't contain themselves either. "We," he said.

I wish I could have been kind to him, in some way. That's what I wanted, when I showed an interest in his house, when I was friendly and cheerful. But I can't give him what he keeps waiting for.

There are other types of men here. I've seen them on the streets, in cafés and coffee shops over the last years. And they've seen me.

Well dressed, well groomed, to all appearances my old self – they've been noticing me for a long time. I've been the one to turn my eyes away, as I was brought up to do. "We," he said. I'm no longer going to turn them away.

Whatever I'm missing, I want to go out and find. Together with someone I choose myself. I can go into a coffee shop again without letting myself be gathered up like wreckage.

I want to get to know men, to find out what they're like, to see if I can love them. Nothing will be like you and me, Lukas, but that's not my intention. These are needy times.

There are lady-killers you couldn't be with in a room for five minutes before they moved in on you. They're everywhere and they're not the ones I'm thinking of.

But what sort of change is happening, has happened, to so many people? Look after your own interests – that's the first law now, for us, and for those we live among.


A mild, quiet day. Misty sunlight. The fragrance of box-wood in the park we walked through, of faded leaves and roses. The sensation of being a leaf yourself, if not as faded, then as torn loose from the place you'd grown up, as whirled away from it — the booty of wind and chance.

New expectations, too.

What I first saw, when we arrived, was the wild splendor of dahlias along the wall, of petunias and snapdragons. Luxuriant clematis on trellises around the little terrace, white clover in the newly mown lawn between the house and the hedge. Out through an open window a flutter of clean curtains. All of it marked by a love of things, a yearning for beauty and good will.

That fine poverty of ours came into my thoughts, though for him this is great prosperity, something he has diligently and laboriously worked for.

As far as I could see the small houses were exactly alike, or almost so. They were all low-roofed, and the sky above high and wide. The difference lay in the gardens, each and every one of which had its own character. I felt right away that his — that ours — was the nicest.

Out on the road children played, looking the way they do in this country: white-blond heads, summer brown fair skin, blue eyes, plump and healthy. Children growing up well, the way they should. Their mothers call them in from playing through windows that let out the smell of good food, as good as it can be nowadays. Well prepared. Frying in butter is something no one does anymore, not even here.

A country without war, a country spared, where, all the same, they have to give up certain things.

I went inside with him, looked around. Furniture and objects quite different than those we grew up with. A few years ago I would have shrugged my shoulders over most of it. Now it was — I believe I felt it was pretty. The things stood there so uprightly, so honestly acquired, so proudly collected. They looked secure.

I didn't have much time to spend there. We looked around a bit, looked at the pretty little kitchen, the two light, low-ceilinged rooms upstairs, the bathroom. Then we went into the garden. But first he asked me with his eyes and I nodded. I picked up a couple of small objects, held them in my hand one after the other and felt that I made a pact with them. And I went into his arms as if it were completely natural.

We sat a while on the terrace. Flags snapped in the wind; from the distance came the sound of a radio. In the neighbor's garden they were moving benches and a table around on the lawn in the shade of the fruit trees. They had visitors, but there was room for everyone; they sat on the benches, drank juice and chatted. I thought, They'll be my neighbors. Now and then an apple dropped into the grass.

He laughed a little apologetically and looked over at his own fruit trees. They were nothing more than tied up sticks with a leaf here and there.

At the streetcar he gripped my hand, hard. Do you think you'll be happy here?

They were words I'd heard before, had answered with a divided mind, with an inner caution I'd glossed over with adjectives. Now I merely answered, Yes, and went into his arms once more, right under the noses of the people who stood waiting. And people stared. They knew him well and wondered where he'd gotten me from.

I didn't care. In a loud, happy voice I said, Till Wednesday.

He's brown and strong, sinewy and thin, a working man. But that's no trifle in this country. It can mean your own house and art hanging on the walls, good art, chosen with understanding. He had two paintings. You would have liked them.

He's not closed up inside himself, like the men of my own class. No — he's open, tender, cheerful. Naïve? Yes, he's naïve. Only naïve people build themselves a home around a dream.

I am, of course, not the first for him. Quite a few times he's kept "steady company," as the saying goes. Not so steady that they were able to come live in his house. I'm allowed to, a position of trust. I'll be careful with things, will remember that they've been obtained by care and sacrifice. That each of them means a victory. I'll try to teach myself to make a little more than an omelette. That will bring some order and equanimity to my life.

He's on leave from the neutrality forces and will soon go back again. We'll have a few days together, then I'll begin to wait, to write to him, to keep the house and garden as well as I can and to look forward to him coming home again.

I may, mayn't I, Lukas? I need to.

Be faithful to a shadow? I know some are, are faithful their whole lives long. But don't you believe that the exiled, and those who were taken away as slaves, that they too in ancient times...?

That they in the end took what life offered them, I mean.

He knows everything. Sympathizing as if it concerned a friend, he listened to what I told him about you. He said, You're free the day you want to be, that's clear. No person owns another. If it turns out that your husband is alive, you may choose again.

He also said, We'll keep trying through the Red Cross. We'll proceed honorably.

Neither of you should hold a grudge against the other, Lukas. Remember that I didn't drift over to him; I steered there as well as I could, across the lonely sea.


I will write a letter, a nice, thankful letter.

Wednesday morning when the sound of the entry door tells me that the man of the house has gone to his office, and the sound of the kitchen door that Mrs. Sjøkvist is off to shop, I'll place it on the table in his study.

I wish I could put inside the letter the strange blend of compassion and gratitude I always felt, along with the stubborn aversion it precipitated, like sediment you throw away.

I won't leave an address. A little cowardly perhaps, but what use is discussion? He'll think, These foreigners – immoral people for the most part. No, in that respect, we're different in this country.

It's a pity; he didn't think that way before. It's my fault.

Lukas, I won't say farewell to you. Deep inside I'll wait for you till death. Yet if you really came one day...

No, now my thoughts trip over each other....

**women in translation**

## An Everyday Story: Norwegian Women's Fiction
*edited by Katherine Hanson*

Norway's tradition of storytelling comes alive in this important anthology of women's prose fiction, the first to appear in English translation. Twenty-four authors are represented, including Camilla Collett, Sigrid Undset, Ebba Haslund and Cécilie Løveid.

*"...An excellent opportunity to sample an interesting, often memorable variety of styles and voices."* — The Los Angeles Times

Paper, $8.95 (ISBN: 0-931188-22-9)
Cloth, $16.95 (ISBN: 0-931188-21-0)

## Early Spring
by Tove Ditlevsen

*translated by Tiina Nunnally*

The memoirs of one of Denmark's best-loved writers.

*"...a poet's book, written with immediacy and radiance."*
— Tillie Olsen
*"...an imagination so literary that it is almost feverish."*
— Publishers Weekly

Paper, $8.95 (ISBN: 0-931188-28-8)
Cloth, $14.95 (ISBN: 0-931188-29-6)

## Egalia's Daughter
by Gerd Brantenberg

*translated by Louis Mackay*

An hilarious satire of the sexes that takes place in Egalia, where the "wim" rule and the "menwim" stay home — and plot liberation.

Paper, $8.95 (ISBN: 0-931188-34-2)
Cloth, $15.95 (ISBN: 0-931188-35-0)

(All prices subject to change without notice.)

Please write to The Seal Press for the most recent list of other women's titles of interest: P.O. Box 13, Seattle, WA 98111.